Tommy Ellis Goes to Sea

Jes Parkin

D0529080

Tommy Ellis Goes to Sea

Copyright © 2014 Jes Parkin

This book is a work of fiction and, except in the case of historical fact, any resemblance to actual persons, living or dead, is purely coincidental.

Published by Stella Books.

Stella Books

ISBN-13: 978-0-9929325-0-3
ISBN-10: 0992932505

In memory of my father,

Eric Smith

from whom I have inherited my love, passion

and respect for the sea.

ACKNOWLEDGEMENTS

My thanks to David Sandell, painter, for allowing me to use his portrayal of the "Stella Altair" on the book cover. David exhibits at the Myton Gallery in Hull.

To Peter O'Connor of BespokeBookCovers.com for designing the cover.

To Claire Wingfield, editor, for her invaluable advice and guidance.

To my family and friends for their love and support

It is 1959 in Hull, a large fishing community on the River Humber in the North East of England. Tommy Ellis is nervously anticipating a new adventure, at sea with his father.

CHAPTER ONE

The great frothy, foamy hands of the watery giant wrapped themselves around him and dragged him down. Fighting for breath, he was gasping, spluttering, and thrashing his arms. He tried to scream, 'Help!', but his mouth filled with the icy cold, salty water as he was spinning round and round. He went under, then came back up, and went under again, kicking his legs and wrestling to get back up again. His clothes were heavy, tugging him under, swirling down in the vortex, but he carried on fighting, even though he felt the strength seeping out of him. A voice inside was yelling, "Dad! Dad!" Down, down he sank, ever deeper into the black depths of the abyss.

. . .

"Wake up Tommy lad, it's time to go."

Tommy shuddered out of his dream, a dream with thunderous, roaring noises, where he was waving

3

his arms around, struggling to breathe, fighting whatever he was being dragged into, yet, as he awoke, he had forgotten what he had been dreaming about. He'd had bad dreams before, but not like this one. What was it? Hot and sweaty, he yawned, stretched and looked at the clock on his bedside table. It was a quarter past three a.m. – the middle of the night. His father was standing by his bed, whispering,

"Sshh. Don't wake your sisters." Before creeping out of the room and down the stairs.

Tommy would have loved to roll over again and go back to sleep, but he knew there was no time to stay in bed. He and his father had to get down to the fish dock and on board so as not to miss the tide. He was shaking, he felt sick and deep inside there was something dark and heavy that worried him. Was he nervous about going to sea, or was it his dream? What had he been dreaming about?

No time to waste. He yawned and stretched again, jumped out of bed, grabbed his clothes and scuttled to the bathroom for a quick wash. He'd had a bath before going to bed so he wasn't dirty. He quickly splashed some water on his face, cleaned his teeth and wet his hair to make it stay down instead of spiking up on the crown. He hated his hair. Once he was ready he went downstairs being careful not to trip over his and his father's kit bags lying ready by the front door in the hallway.

His mother was also up and in the kitchen where she'd made a pot of tea and was toasting bread under the grill. Tommy liked toast for breakfast, especially if it had lots of butter and lashings of orange marmalade. He could smell the bread toasting and was already licking his lips in anticipation. He sat at the kitchen table while his mother shuffled about in her pink fluffy slippers, pink silky dressing gown, and a chiffon scarf wrapped around her head to cover her hair curlers. He poured tea into his mug and looked around, knowing that it would be three weeks before he'd be back here again. His eyes fell on the washing machine. His mum had one of those new fangled twin-tubs, but no way would it be used today.

5

Trawler families were superstitious and neither wives nor mothers ever did the washing on the day their men sailed. They said it was like washing them away. Tommy shuddered.

"Are you cold pet?"

His mother, noticing him shake, sounded worried.

"No, I'm alright," he replied.

Tommy Ellis was a bright lad from Hull who had always done well at school. He was a quiet boy, not as tall as his some of his school friends who were growing rapidly. He had short, straight, dark brown hair which always stuck up on the top, even though he tried to plaster it down with water every morning. A year ago he had passed his Eleven Plus examination and had just finished his first year at Kingston High School on Pickering Road. He liked sport and had already been selected to play on the school football team. His mother and father were very proud of him and, now that he was growing up, his Dad said that he would take him on a trip to sea, a 'pleasure trip', during the school summer holidays. A huge adventure for a school boy.

6

Nobody in his class at school had ever been to sea, and on the last day at the end of term, his friends all said they would like to be going with him and wished him good luck. Tommy went home from school looking forward. He was lightheaded and felt he was walking on air. But he was also worried and a bit scared. This was a massive change from what he usually did during the six week summer break. Apart from playing out with his friends, he, his mother and his two sisters always went to Withernsea for a week to stay in their Uncle Jim and Aunty Betty's caravan. He had looked forward to this holiday year after year, but this year was different. This year he would be joining a man's world. His father's world.

Tommy didn't know his father very well at all. He was the man he and his sisters called Dad, who came home for a couple of days every three weeks, then went back to sea again. Some of his school friends had fathers who came home from work every evening and helped them with their homework, fathers who would play football with

7

them, or get them to help with jobs around the house or in the garden. Would he get to know his father better during this trip? He hoped so.

"Taxi's here."

The sound of his father's voice shook him out of his daydreaming. He started to shake and he felt sick again as he got up from his chair. What was that dream about? His mother hugged him tightly, which was something she rarely did now that he was nearly grown. She tried to sound excited,

"You be a good lad now. See you when you get back. Oh, and by the way, I've put some paper bags in your kit bag, in case you get an asthma attack."
He hadn't had an asthma attack for ages and he only ever had one when he was near animals. They found out he was allergic to the fur when he was about five and that was why he couldn't have a dog or a guinea pig.

"Have a nice holiday in Withernsea, Mum," he replied bashfully.

"We don't have animals on board, except for some of the deck hands that is," his father added, swinging his bag over his shoulder and chuckling as he walked down the path. Tommy's father had thick greying hair with a parting down the left side and it was always combed into place with special hair grease. Tommy recognised the distinct musky fragrance of the Brylcream that he bought him for Christmas every year. He wasn't a very tall man, but he was stout with broad shoulders, solid arms, shovel-like hands, and fingers like thick sausages. Tommy felt a lump in his throat and fought back the tears that were prickling his eyes as he picked up his kit bag and walked out through the door, following his father to the taxi which had parked at the kerb outside their house.

Once the taxi had set off, Tommy yawned so hard he felt his lips would split at the corners. He had never been up this early before. Tommy and his father sat in silence, each looking out of the taxi window; Tommy, with both hands on his lap, and his father with his elbow against the taxi door, his hand cupping his chin. The streets they had ridden along close to home had been quiet and deserted,

9

but as they got closer to Hessle Road he could see there was more and more movement of people, trucks and taxis. The other taxis were going in the same direction as they were and Tommy wondered if any of the men inside were going on the same trawler as he was.

They drove along West Dock Avenue where they used to live, past their old house, one of many small, crowded, terraced houses, and Tommy's old school. He recognized the houses of some of their old neighbours. The Wilkinsons who lived at number 12 with a bright red door, the Hudsons who had six children, and the Robsons. Steve Robson was Tommy's best friend before they moved away, but he didn't see him these days. He hoped he would see Steve again one day. Tommy remembered living in the old house where he sometimes saw the taxis go by taking the men to sea. Now it was his turn to go.

As they reached the end of the street, they entered the tunnel which would take them onto the fish dock. He had been through this tunnel before on many occasions when, with his mother and two sisters, he went to wait for his father's trawler to come home after a trip. This time it was different. While they were driving through the tunnel, the sound of the taxi's engine echoed loudly, as did the sound of the clogs of the men going to work. Their clogs were very different to the clogs worn by people in Holland. The Dutch clogs were the slip on kind, made only of wood. The clogs worn by the fish dock workers looked like boots, laced up leather on the top, thick, wooden soles and metal tips nailed under the soles which gave them the familiar clip clop sound as the men walked. The young lad's heart was leaping up into the back of his throat. He was on the road of no return. He clasped his hands together tightly so as to hide his shaking, hoping his father would not notice.

Coming out of the tunnel at the other side, they were in a different world. St. Andrew's Dock. Tommy opened his mouth wide and gasped with amazement. It was the first time he had been there when the trawlers were getting ready to sail. It was as busy as the town centre on a Saturday afternoon. There were cars, lorries, railway carriages, men and boys pushing barrows here and there, people dashing about shouting to each other. So much noise. Tommy looked at his watch. Half past four. He hadn't known before that there was such a lot of hustle and bustle on the dock at this time of the morning. There were Bobbers with heavy clogs on their feet clattering along the cobble stones, rushing to unload the fish just landed from the trawlers which had recently docked, so as to make the morning market; filleters busily flashing their knives through the fish as quickly as they could as the containers, or kits, used to unload the fish, came ashore one after the other. It was continuous buzzing, banging and clattering noises. Then, of course, there were the taxis, dozens of them. Their taxi joined a queue and slowly edged along passing some buildings on the left.

"You do know you won't be getting any special treatment don't you lad? You're just another member of the crew – like everybody else. You'll have your jobs to do," his father said with a serious tone to his voice.

"Yes Dad, I'll do my best." Tommy hadn't expected to hear those words, but what did he expect? He really didn't know.

Tommy saw a man carrying a clip board and a pen in his hand. He was tall and lean looking, wearing a flat cap, thick black rimmed spectacles and, even though it was the month of July, he wore a sheepskin jacket.

"That's Bert Cooper, the company runner," his father said. "He checks that everyone who has signed on arrives on board in time to catch the tide."

He wound down the window and shouted to the man. Bert came over straight away saying,

"Morning Skipper. Nearly everyone on board, just two deck hands missing."

"Have you got my lad's stuff?" Tommy's father asked.

"Yes, just coming, Skipper." He turned his head and shouted,

"George, come over here with that stuff will you."

Another man approached the taxi. Tommy's father opened the door and into the taxi came a rough cotton sack filled with straw, which was really to be his mattress, a pair of long rubber boots and other articles of clothing Tommy didn't recognize. His father took some money out of his wallet and gave it to Bert, who promptly doffed his cap saying,

"Anything to oblige Skipper."

A man doffing his cap to his father? He hadn't realized that his father was of such high standing. Tommy looked questioningly at his father, who said,

"Just a few things you'll be needing for the trip. Fishermen have to buy their own gear, even the mattress they sleep on."

This was news to Tommy. Fancy having to buy your own mattress. He hadn't expected that at all.

"Is that it Skipper?" The taxi driver asked.

"Yes, that's it. Off we go."

The taxi pulled out of the queue and made its way to the far side of the dock, the south side, weaving its way through groups of men, trucks and other taxis. Tommy could see a lot of trawlers at the quayside, two or three abreast, belching smoke from their funnels. The funnels were different colours, depending on who the trawler owners were. It was tide time and they were all waiting to sail through the lock, down the River Humber, and out into the North Sea. Tommy looked around. He saw other taxis dropping men off, and groups of men standing around at the quayside, kit bags by their feet, while they chatted amongst themselves. They pulled up alongside the Stella Vega, a side-winding trawler, and got out. There were other trawlers with the word 'Stella' in front of their name. The Stella Arcturus and the Stella Antares were tied up at the quayside not far from the Stella Vega. All the trawlers of the Charleson-Smith Company were named after stars and Stella means star. In fact, all the Stella trawlers had a star on the bow.

Tommy took a deep breath as he looked up at the ship. It looked big from the quayside, bigger than he had expected anyway. The pointed bow with the fo'c'sle, the raised deck area at the front of a ship,

15

and the rounded stern looked to be much higher than the centre part, the waist of the vessel, where the bridge rose proudly from the deck. The hull was painted black and towards the bows he read the number H494 followed by the name 'Stella Vega'. He looked up at the funnel, painted white with two black bands near the top, the company colours. He thought about his dream again. It had scared him, but what was it? Was it something to do with his trip? Was it a message? He felt a chill run across his shoulders and down his spine.

CHAPTER TWO

The driver took his father's kit bag and carried it on board for him. Tommy looked at him and waited.

"I'm the skipper. You carry your own."

As soon as they climbed on board, they were approached by a grey-haired man who looked much older than Tommy's father. He wasn't very tall, in fact, not much taller than Tommy, who was just five foot. His wrinkles were deep and looked like the furrows in a farmer's field, and his face was like tough old leather. His bare forearms were full of scars.

"Is this the lad then?" The older man asked.

"This is 'im," his father replied before turning to his son,

"Tommy, this is Bob Fletcher, the Cook. One of your jobs will be helping him while you're on board."

Remembering his manners, Tommy said,

17

"How do you do Mr Fletcher?"

The Cook squinted his eyes and looked him up and down saying,

"Come with me."

Tommy turned to look at his father, who said,

"Go on. You'll be alright. Cook'll look after you."

He picked up his bag and his mattress, his father placing the other items on the pile in his arms, and, with a lump in his throat and his chin resting on top of the pile so that it wouldn't topple over, he struggled through the doorway to the inside of the ship. The light was much brighter inside than outside, brighter than he had expected, and it took Tommy's eyes a few seconds to get used to the change. He came to the top of a steep staircase. Cook was standing at the bottom telling him to walk down backwards. Tommy hesitated, not knowing how he was going to get down with all his things.

"Hurry up posh lad," the Cook shouted, "or is it daft lad? Yeah, you're just a daft lad. Chuck everything down and pick it up at the bottom."

Tommy jerked his head and fixed his eyes on the

Cook. This man had just called him 'daft lad'. He wanted to yell at him, "I'm not a daft lad", but remembered he had always been taught that it's wrong to answer back to adults. So, he did as he was told and, after picking his things up again and staggering along the passageway, he followed Cook to where he was standing by an open door.

"You're in here," he growled.

Tommy wrinkled his nose as he entered the grubby little room. It was triangular shaped, a wooden bunk on two sides, meeting at the far end, and the ceiling wasn't as high as the ceiling out in the passageway. There were no cupboards, just a shelf above the bunks. And what was that smell? It smelt like his friend's father's garage, a mixture of paint and oil. He looked around, but there was no window.

"A pleasure trip eh?" Cook laughed. "You can be sure there'll not be much pleasure for you, daft lad. Dump your stuff then come up to the galley. There's work to be done."

He'd been called 'daft lad' again. He wanted to

19

challenge this man, but thought better of it. He had to work with these people.

"Where's the galley?" he asked.

"Follow your nose," was the cook's brusque reply.

What did he mean, "Follow your nose"? This was not a good start. He didn't like Bob Fletcher, and he was sure Bob Fletcher didn't like him. Feeling downhearted he began to wish he'd stayed at home.

Tommy lifted his mattress onto the bunk on the opposite wall, together with his kit bag and the new articles of clothing his father had arranged for him. The rubber boots were very high and he knew they would reach the tops of his legs. There was a pair of thick, heavy trousers and an oilskin tunic. He wondered why he would need those if he was going to be helping the cook in the galley. When he opened his bag he pulled out the paper bags his mother had packed for him and hid them under the mattress feeling sure they wouldn't be needed. Then there were two pairs of thick woollen socks his mother had knitted for him as well as a thick

20

guernsey. He didn't understand why he would need all this thick, heavy clothing. It was summer after all. He was about to go and find his way to the galley when another boy came in.

"Who are you?" the boy asked.

"Tommy, Tommy Ellis."

He saw the boy was quite a bit taller than him and stocky. He had a cheeky grin and his fair hair had been scraped back at the sides with grease and a floppy quiff hung down over his forehead. His eyes were bright blue and twinkled under the electric light of the cabin. He jauntily leant against the door jamb with his hands in his trouser pockets. He was wearing pale blue jeans which seemed to match the colour of his eyes, a wide black belt with a large buckle, and a white shirt open at the neck showing a white tee shirt underneath.

"Oh, the skipper's lad. Come to spy on us have you?" The newcomer was no longer grinning.

Tommy took a step back, stunned, not expecting a comment like that.

"No. I've come for a trip and I've been told I'll

be working with the cook," he replied, not understanding why this boy would be so suspicious of him.

"Oh, a pleasure tripper." The newcomer looked down his nose. "Well, we'll see, but watch your back anyway. Watch out especially for the Gallagher brothers, Sid and Stan. They're a couple of deck hands and they're a nasty, rough lot."

Tommy knew that some of the fishermen were rough and ready and would sometimes fight with each other. He decided he would try to stay out of their way.

"My name's Mike by the way. Mike Beech. I'm the Deckie Learner." Reaching out to shake Tommy's hand.

The name rang a bell with Tommy so he asked,

"Do you live down West Dock Avenue?"

"Yeah. And you used to live there too. I remember when you moved away. I was still at school and you were just a little kid. You used to be in the same class as my sister, Angela."

"Yes, I remember Angela Beech." He thought

22

back to West Dock Avenue School and the fair haired girl with freckles who always wanted to join in with the boys' games at play time.

"Are you in this cabin too?" Tommy asked feeling that maybe he might make a friend.
Mike curled his top lip upwards, wrinkled his nose and replied,

"Yeah, so make sure your stuff doesn't get mixed up with mine." Mike was showing his authority as the older and more experienced crew member.

"Well," Tommy said trying to sound enthusiastic, "I'd best get going. I've got to find the galley."

"Good luck," Mike replied with that cheeky grin of his. "Rather you than me."

As Tommy went back into the passageway, he realized that he had been hearing a strange noise since arriving on board, a noise that seemed to make everything vibrate. The noise was that of the engines. It was a deep, throbbing sound which pulsated throughout the ship. A continuous, massaging rhythm, the heartbeat of the ship, at the same time matching his own heartbeat.

23

He did as Cook said and followed his nose to the galley. It was easy as he couldn't mistake the smell of freshly baked bread.

The galley on board ship is the kitchen, and it was very different to his mother's kitchen back home. (He thought about his mother for a moment and wondered if she'd gone back to bed.) It was much smaller. There was a large iron stove over to one side, with bars in front of it just a bit higher than the stove itself. There was a small door below the bars which was open and inside was a roaring fire. It reminded Tommy of his grandma's old-fashioned fireplace with an oven at the side of it. On the opposite side there was a large sink and there were cupboards and drawers around the walls. There was a hatchway in one of the walls and he wondered what was on the other side. Right in the centre of the galley was an iron rail with some tea towels hanging over it.

As well as the smell of fresh bread, Tommy could now smell the bacon that was frying in a large pan on the stove. There were about a dozen eggs in

24

another large frying pan as well as a big pan of beans at the back of the cooker.

Cook was standing by the sink, but soon turned round when Tommy entered the galley.

"Go in the mess next door," the Cook growled while pointing to the wall with a hatch, "and make sure the tables are set and the tea's mashing."

There were four men sitting at one of the tables. They had just finished their breakfasts and were laughing and joking, but, as soon as Tommy walked in they stopped their talking and turned to look at him. One leaned towards another and whispered, "Skipper's lad." All four looked away from him, picked up some magazines and pretended to read. One of them mumbled,

"We'd better watch our P's and Q's this trip then."

Tommy hadn't expected to make friends with everybody, but he didn't think he would be given such a cold reception. He decided to ignore them and checked that every place setting had a knife, fork, spoon, a plate and a mug. Over by the hatch

25

was a very large teapot, so he lifted the lid and stirred the tea inside, replacing the lid when he had finished. As he left the mess he heard the men laugh out loud. He realized he was going to have to have his wits about him as he didn't want to be made to look stupid.

Cook was waiting for him back in the galley.

"If you want any breakfast get it yourself," he snapped.

Tommy's mouth was watering as the smell of bacon was filling his nose, so he muttered a quiet,

"Thank you."

The bread was already cut into thick, doorstep size slices. He covered two slices with butter, and made the biggest bacon sandwich he had ever seen. He took it into the mess and, ignoring the men in there, sat down and ate his breakfast. The bacon was greasy and the melting butter dripped out of his sandwich onto his plate. His mother would have chowed at him and told him he was eating like a pig, but he didn't care. One of the men said,

"Don't they feed you at home, lad?" and the

others laughed.

Cook poked his head through the hatch between the galley and the mess,

"Skipper'll be ready for his tea and we don't want to keep him waiting do we daft lad? Here, take this," he said passing a very large metal teapot to Tommy, "and here's a couple a packets of tea and a bottle of milk. Don't drop anything."

Tommy picked up the items and looked at Cook who smirked at him saying,

"You don't know where to go do you daft lad?" grinning at the other men in the mess.

"Up the stairs at yon end, and onto the bridge. He'll be in the wheelhouse," then shouted as Tommy started on his way, "and don't get lost."

Tommy wasn't used to being spoken to in this way and it made him uncomfortable. He hoped it wouldn't go on for the whole trip, but what could he do? Maybe if he showed Cook that he could work as hard as anybody else that would help? He had to try and change things round. Three weeks of this treatment was going to be awful.

27

As Tommy was striding along the passage and before he got to the stairs, his chest suddenly felt tight and he started to wheeze. He stopped for a second, not expecting this to happen, then carried on and struggled to breathe as he climbed the stairs. He entered the wheelhouse with a clatter, dropping the teapot, but, luckily, not the bottle of milk. His father, who was standing at the opposite side of the bridge came bounding over, hissing,

"What on earth's the matter with you?"

He took the bottle of milk from Tommy and placed it on a shelf nearby. Tommy couldn't answer as he was trying to breathe. His father dragged him into the chart room, which was just through a doorway on the back wall, sat him down on the settee and kneeling in front of him with his hands on his shoulders, repeated,

"Blow! Blow! Blow!"

As he was fighting for breath, Tommy heard his father and, remembering the exercise, pretended to blow up balloons as hard as he could, which would make him take in deep breaths. He did as he was

28

told, but his chest hurt so much. After about ten minutes, his breathing became normal again. He looked up at his father and said,

"Sorry dad."

His father, standing in front of him, hands on hips, shook his head,

"We haven't even set off yet. What's brought this on?"

"I don't know Dad. I was just walking along the passage and it happened," Tommy replied meekly. He had hoped to get to know his father better, and for them to become friends, but this wasn't going to help.

"Well, I haven't time for this now," his father said impatiently, "we're sailing in a couple of minutes. You can stand on the bridge for now and watch as we go through the lock."

When Tommy went back through to the bridge he saw there was a man at the wheel. He didn't speak to Tommy, just glared at him through steely eyes. He had a long, pointed nose that curved down as if trying to reach his up-turned pointed chin. Tommy didn't like the look of this man, but smiled and nodded to him before turning to look out of the window. On the fo'c'sle, there were a group of men waiting for orders. They were not wearing working clothes, they were dressed in their shore suits. The suits of many trawlermen were unlike the suits worn by other men around the city. The trawlermen's suits often had pleats at the back of the jacket and slit, half-moon shaped pockets on the breast. The trousers had a high close fitting cummerbund type waistband and the legs flared out widely to the ground. Often they were in pale colours like pearl grey or powder blue, but sometimes you would see one in black. Yes, they were very distinctive and were worn with pride. Tommy's father didn't own a trawler suit though. He preferred a more classic style, or was it because of his status as Skipper, not wanting to resemble a Deck Hand?

"Stand by!" bellowed Tommy's father, making him jump.

Looking out of the window, Tommy could see the men on the fo'c'sle holding a very large rope.

30

There were also two men on the quayside holding the same rope.

"Away for'ard. Away aft," his father shouted again. Tommy knew that for'ard meant the front of the ship and aft was at the back. Tommy stretched his neck forward, closer to the window, hoping to get a better view of what was going on. The men on the quayside let go of their rope which fell between the ship and quay. He imagined that the same was happening aft. His father turned to him and said,

"Alright lad?"

Tommy nodded, smiling, holding his head up, hoping no one would notice how nervous he was. His father then said,

"Right Gallagher, take her through the lock."

To which the man at the wheel promptly replied, "Aye aye Skipper."

Tommy's heart skipped a beat. Gallagher. Mike had told him to watch out for the Gallagher brothers. He tried to look at the man without turning his head. His sleeves were rolled up to the

31

elbow and he had a big tattoo on his forearm, a red heart with a dagger passing through it. Tommy decided he would try to stay away from this mean looking man. He tried to keep very still and stop fidgeting as he stood at the far corner of the bridge, looking out of the window. The Stella Vega edged her way through into the lock and was followed by another trawler before the gates were closed behind them. It wasn't very long, maybe about ten minutes, before the gates in front of them opened and they made their way out into the River Humber. The Skipper gave instructions to Gallagher and returned to the chart room.

Tommy looked around at the unfamiliar surroundings. The wheelhouse was filled with instruments, both under the windows and along the back wall. Gallagher turned to look at him and said through a half smile with no teeth,

"You don't have to stay up here all day, you know."

Tommy saw the man's mouth was smiling but his eyes weren't. He looked back at him and asked,

"Will it be alright if I go and have a look around?"

"Yeah, go on.   Mind you don't get lost," Gallagher replied sniggering.

Tommy imagined that everybody on board thought he was just a stupid little boy, a daft lad. He hoped he would be able to change their minds, to show them that he could work hard and be accepted as just another member of the crew. Head held low, he left the bridge.

With a heavy heart, and feeling very lonely, Tommy stood on the deck below the bridge as the Stella Vega started to make its way down the River Humber towards the North Sea. It had just turned daylight so he could see the shore clearly. He recognized the strange wing-shaped chimney pots of the smoke houses which were just off Hessle Road. He had seen them from the road many times, but had not really noticed them as they had always been part of the Hessle Road landscape as he was growing up. They sailed past William Wright and Albert Docks and came level with Victoria Pier where the 'Wingfield Castle', the New Holland ferry, had recently tied up and the passengers were disembarking, going to their place of work. He remembered the previous year when he and his family went on the ferry to New Holland in Lincolnshire, where they caught a train to Cleethorpes to spend a day at the seaside. It was a change from Hornsea, Withernsea or Bridlington, and it was a long way, but he enjoyed the ferry crossing. He could see Holy Trinity Church and King Billy, the golden statue of the king on his horse which sat on top of the toilets. He wondered what King Billy thought of being placed on the roof of the Gentlemen's public toilets. Queen Victoria was also sitting on the roof of the public toilets in Queen Victoria Square in front of the City Hall. He chuckled to himself thinking, 'I bet they don't like that.'

They passed the mouth of the River Hull where he could see a few barges being loaded next to Ranks Flour Mill, and other barges coming down the river from the mills and factories at Stoneferry. He thought that these people must have been up very early like him. Then they sailed past Victoria Dock where there were ships unloading timber. He had heard grown-ups refer to Victoria Dock as the 'Red Square' because of the large number of Russian ships that docked there. After that came Alexander Dock, then King George Dock. There were lots of big cargo ships in these docks, bigger than his father's trawler. They sailed all around the world and he wondered what it would be like to travel to far off countries like India or China or South America. Places he had read about in his school books, and dreamed of visiting one day.

"I've been looking all over the place for you. Thought you might have jumped ship and gone home crying to your Mummy."

Tommy nearly jumped out of his skin as Cook came up behind him.

"Do you know how to peel taties?"

"Yes," Tommy replied squinting his eyes at this grumpy little man.

"Well come on then, let's be having you."

Tommy followed Cook into the storeroom in the

35

corner of the galley where he saw a large bin full of potatoes.

"You can sit outside to do them if you like," Cook said. "there isn't much room in here." He held his hand out to Tommy saying, "Here's a knife. Mind you don't cut yourself like a daft lad."

"How many do you want peeling?" asked Tommy curtly, hoping that the Cook would realize he was annoyed at being called 'daft lad'.

"All of 'em," replied Cook, chuckling to himself.

Tommy thought it would take him ages, but he settled himself out on the deck, just outside the door with his bin of potatoes and his knife and started peeling. They had just sailed past Paull where he could see the short, stumpy, white lighthouse. The knife was very sharp therefore he worked slowly so as not to cut his fingers. After he had peeled about half a dozen, he was joined by another lad he hadn't seen before.

"Hiya. I've come to give you a hand." Tommy was shocked to hear such a deep, croaky voice. "I'm Brian, the Galley Boy. I've just finished

36

sorting out the stores, putting stuff away for the trip. Taties is usually my job, and it takes ages on your own."

"Thanks. I'm Tommy."

"Yeah, I know who you are. Mike, the Deckie Learner, told me. Cook'll be calling *you* 'daft lad' now, instead of me," Brian said with a deep throaty chuckle.

"I thought he was picking on me," Tommy said.

"He does that with any new lad. Likes to think he's in charge. Well, I suppose he is in the galley. He's alright once you get to know him."

Tommy wasn't so sure.

Both boys laughed and carried on with the peeling. Brian looked about fifteen. He wasn't very tall and he was skinny, not the type of build you would expect to have such a deep voice. He had short, brown hair, freckles across his nose and along his cheekbones, and when he smiled you could see his two front teeth were crooked. He was wearing a cream coloured apron that had been folded over a couple of times round the waist as it

37

must have been too long for him. There were also some stains on the apron which had not washed out. The two boys chatted while peeling the potatoes and Tommy was glad that he liked Brian as they would be seeing a lot of each other during the trip. While they were peeling away at the potatoes, Brian asked,

"Can you keep a secret?"

To which Tommy eagerly replied,

"Yes, I can."

Brian pondered for a while, then said,

"No. It doesn't matter."

"Go on. I won't tell. Promise."

Brian thought for a few more seconds then said,

"No, not now. I'll tell you later."

Tommy was impatient to know what Brian's secret was, but said nothing more as he didn't want him to change his mind about trusting him. He was happy he had found somebody who would talk to him and treat him like a friend. Three weeks was a long time and with Brian, the Galley Boy on his side, and maybe Mike, the Deckie Learner, it wouldn't be too bad, would it?

CHAPTER THREE

They sailed out of the River Humber and into the North Sea. Tommy felt the roll of the ship over the gentle swell of the waves and a stronger vibration as the engines turned to full speed. The bow was lifted up over the bigger waves, down into the dips, then up again on the next wave. The sea wasn't rough, but it was much more powerful than the river.

Tommy took in deep breaths so as to savour the fresh, salty sea air, but what was the matter with his tummy? He could taste his breakfast again. Oh no, he didn't want to be sea sick. He took in long, deep breaths, hoping the feeling would pass, but it all got too much for him. He dropped his knife as he jumped up, and in one leap grabbed the side of the ship with both hands. He hung his head over the side, started to heave, threw up the remains of his bacon sandwich and watched it disappear into the water below. He heard Brian laughing behind him and felt ashamed.

39

"Don't worry Tommy," said Brian. "It happens to the best of us. The bosun's been going to sea for years and he always throws up the first day out. You'll get used to it. Anyway," he continued, "if you've finished being sick, we've still got these taties to peel. Better get a move on or Cook will have our guts for garters."

After he and Brian had finished peeling the potatoes and taken them into the galley for the Cook, Tommy went back up onto the bridge where another of the deck hands was at the wheel, and his father was checking some charts in the chart room. The deck hand didn't acknowledge Tommy, which was what he expected, so he went and stood by his father. He glanced down at the charts and asked,

"Where are we going?"

"Bear Island," his father replied pointing to a place on the chart.

"How long will it take us to get there?"

"Four or five days. Depends on the weather." Tommy's father then turned to a tape recorder which was fastened onto a shelf. He took a reel out

40

of a drawer, wound it into position and switched it on. Country and Western music started blaring out over the loud speakers and Tommy could hear the cheers from the crew. He went to the bridge window and looked out, down onto the deck. He could see a man was giving orders to others as they were busying themselves securing nets and other items so they would be ready when they started fishing. They had all changed their clothes and were wearing guernseys, fearnought trousers and their sea boots. He noticed Mike, the Deckie Learner, who had also changed into the same type of clothing, holding what looked like a tin of paint and a piece of cloth. He asked his father what Mike was painting and his father chuckled and replied,

"He's not painting, he's greasing the brass work. Why don't you get changed and go and give him a hand. I'll tell the Mate you'll be on deck in a minute."

Tommy didn't understand why Mike would be greasing brass work, but didn't ask as he could see his father was busy and he didn't want to pester him

41

with questions. So, off he went to get changed. Although they were not very far north, there was a slight chill in the air blowing off the sea and he was glad to don his new guernsey. But, on his way to his cabin, as he was walking down the same passageway as before, his chest felt tight again and he started to wheeze. Luckily his cabin was not far away and when he got there, he grabbed one of the paper bags from under his mattress, and, holding it to his mouth, breathed heavily in, out, in, out, inflating and deflating the paper bag until his chest felt easier and he was able to breathe normally again. There was something in that passageway that gave him an asthma attack, but what? He decided that he would keep a paper bag in his trouser pocket at all times, just in case. He didn't want to say anything to his father as he didn't want him to regret bringing him on board.

To get out on deck he had to go back the same way, but this time, before he left the cabin, he took a deep breath, put his hand over his mouth and nose, and ran as fast as he could to the far end.

On the deck, some of the men were singing "Yippee ay ehhhh, Yippee ay oooooo" in time to the music while they worked. Tommy liked cowboy songs too.

"Hiya Mike, I've come to help," Tommy said as he steadied his feet on the deck, legs slightly apart, negotiating the steady roll of the ship.

"'bout time too," Mike grunted, "go to the engine room and ask for a tin of bollard grease."

"Bollard grease?" Tommy asked, checking that he'd understood.

"Yeah. And tell them you want it for me."

When Tommy opened the engine room door the noise was so loud it nearly knocked him over. He felt the heat and the strong smell of oil and paint hit the back of his throat as he gasped. The engine room looked like a big cave going from the top to the bottom of the ship. At the bottom he could see the huge engines and there were metal walkways all around and metal ladders going down to the bottom. He was glad he wasn't working in there. A man wearing a dirty, grey boiler suit came to him and shouted, but Tommy couldn't hear what he was saying and just shook his head. The man tossed his head impatiently and leaned in towards Tommy's face mouthing slowly so that he could understand,

"What – do - you - want?"

Tommy got that, and slowly mouthed back,

"Bollard - grease," and remembering Mike's words, mouthed, "for - Deckie."

The man beckoned Tommy to follow him and gave him a large tin, like a massive tin of paint. It was heavy, but Tommy got a good strong hold of it, nodded a 'thank - you' and left the engine room. What a relief to be away from that dreadful noise and the heat. He wondered if the engineers ever went deaf.

Back on deck, Mike, the Deckie, took a knife out of his pocket and opened the tin saying,

"Good job you got changed."

Mike handed him a cloth and told him to spread the grease around the port holes along the deck. Using the cloth, and with a look of disgust on his face, Tommy put his hand inside the tin into what was

44

like thick, sticky, gluey treacle. Yuk!

Mike laughed,

"You should be here in winter when the freezing cold makes it all hard like toffee. That's when we have to keep taking it to the galley to put on the stove to melt it down again."

Tommy worked along the portholes on the port side of the ship while Mike was greasing other parts. Again no one spoke to him, so he got on with the job. As he worked he thought about Brian and wondered about the secret he'd mentioned. He also wondered how he was going to stop Cook calling him 'daft lad'. After what must have been an hour, or maybe more, he was told to go to the galley as he was needed there. Someone standing close by whispered,

"Good job, lad."

Tommy turned to see Mike smiling at him, so he smiled back and said,

"Thanks." Glad to know he had another friend.

Back in the galley, there was a large pan on the stove and a smell of cooking wafted through the air.

45

It made his mouth water, but he decided to give lunch a miss as his tummy was still feeling a bit funny. The cook was making shackles, the name for stew on board trawlers, and the fresh bread made that morning would be used to mop up the gravy when the meat and vegetables had been eaten. There would be rice pudding for afters. Tommy was tempted by the rice pudding as it was his favourite at home, but thought maybe next time. He didn't want to be sick again.

"That tea in there'll be stewed. Make a fresh pot, if you can manage it daft lad."

He turned to glare at Cook, who followed with,

"Well, what you waiting for?"

Again Tommy wanted to say something, but thought better of it as he didn't want to make trouble for himself or Cook. So, he went next door into the mess to check the teapot and, sure enough, the tea was not only stewed and black, it was nearly cold. By the time he returned with a fresh pot, some of the men had come in for their dinners. Brian, the Galley Boy, had also come into the mess

46

and it was his job to serve the shackles. Tommy made another pot of tea and took it to the officers' mess which was just on the opposite side of the passage. Cook was serving the officers the same food as the crew, so, to keep out of everybody's way, Tommy went back into the galley and washed some dishes. When he had finished, his father invited him to sit with him, the Mate and the Radio Operator for a cup of tea.

The three men were discussing the trip and various positions around the coast of Bear Island. They looked from one to the other as they spoke. They talked about the time of year and where the fish should be at this time. They talked about the number of kits, the drum shaped metal containers used to transport the fish, they had landed the previous trip from White Sea, and that the shoals should now be moving north-west towards Bear Island. All three had an excited tone to their voices. There was no talk of home, their families or anything else that was happening back in Hull, or anywhere else for that matter. In fact, World War

Three could have broken out, but all they were interested in was going out to get that fish.

As the officers were leaving the mess, Tommy's father turned to him and said quietly,

"When you've finished helping Cook clear up in the galley, come up on the bridge, you can give me a hand." Winking at his son as he left. Tommy grinned from ear to ear thinking, 'At last, I'll be doing something with my Dad.'

He took all the empty plates from the officers' mess and the crew mess into the galley where Cook gave him an old apron to wear whilst he was washing up. When he did the washing up at home, he sometimes left the clean dishes on the draining board to dry before he, or more often than not his mother, would put them away. But here on board, all the dishes, cutlery, pots and pans were dried and put away securely as soon as they were washed. They had to be secured so they wouldn't be thrown around when the sea was choppy. When he had finished he told Cook he was going up to the bridge. Cook turned to look at him and grunted something

48

Tommy didn't understand.

"What?" Tommy asked, wanting Cook to see he was listening.

But Cook didn't speak, he just impatiently waved Tommy away with his hand without looking at him. Tommy decided to ignore him and turned around leaving the galley.

CHAPTER FOUR

Tommy found his father talking to Norman, the Radio Operator. Norman was standing in the doorway between the wheelhouse and the chart room and his father was at the wheel.

"Oh, here you are. Come here and I'll show you what to do."

Tommy went over to where his father was standing in the central area of the bridge.

"You can take the wheel for a while. Now, this is the compass," he said pointing to an instrument just behind the wheel, "the needle should be pointing towards the direction we are sailing. When you move the wheel the needle changes to point in another direction. I've written down here the course we are following, so you make sure you keep us going in the right direction. Have you got that?"

"Yes, I've got it. Does that mean I'll be steering the ship?" Tommy asked, not believing the great responsibility he had been given.

"Yes, son. Just keep the needle on those numbers. I'll be in the chart room, right behind you, if you need anything," his father replied, leaving Tommy alone on the bridge, the wheel in his hands and heart pounding out of his chest.

Tommy felt ten feet tall. He looked out of the bridge window in front of him, as far as where the sea met the cloudless sky on the horizon. The sea was a deep shade of blue and there were little white crests of waves breaking on the surface. He watched as the bow rose up over the waves and felt that he was doing the pushing, thinking, "come on, come on," then, "weeeee" as they dropped down into the dip. Over and over again, rising and falling, rising and falling. Down on the deck the crew were busy sorting the nets and the 20 inch steel bobbins that ran nearly the full length of the bulwarks. He saw Mike, the Deckie Learner, still with his tin of bollard grease and a filthy rag in his hand. He checked the compass and was relieved to see he was still on course. Standing alone on the bridge, the wheel in his hands, he felt in charge, not

51

only of the ship, but of everybody on board. He thought, 'If Cook could see me now, he wouldn't call me daft lad.'

He had never felt so happy. He started to whistle, but as he did, his father bounded onto the bridge shouting,

"Shut up!"

Tommy jumped and let go of the wheel as his father took him by the shoulders and yelled in his face,

"You never, never whistle on board a ship. Do you hear?"

"Yes, Dad. Sorry, Dad," Tommy replied not understanding what he had done wrong, and mortified he had upset his father.

"It's a good job only me and Norman heard you. If anybody else had heard, you'd have been over the side in a flash. Now don't do it again," and dismissing him said, "Go and see if you're needed in the galley."

With his head held low and his heart in his boots, he again said, "Sorry," and made his way out of the wheelhouse and down the stairs. He wanted to cry but managed not to as he didn't want others to see he was upset. It would probably get back to Cook and he would start to call him 'cry baby' as well as 'daft lad' and that wouldn't do.

He didn't go straight to the galley. He went to his cabin and lay down on his bunk. What had he done wrong? The door was flung open and the Deckie, Mike, walked in.

"What's up with you?"

"Nothing," Tommy murmured turning his face to the wall.

"Something's up. You've got a face like a wet weekend."

Tommy wanted to ask Mike about the whistling, but remembering his father's words about being thrown overboard, he just said,

"Feeling a bit sea sick, that's all."

Mike smiled,

"You'll get over it. It happens to me sometimes, so you're not on your own."

Mike picked up a pair of gloves and winked at Tommy as he left the cabin. Tommy stayed for a

53

little while longer, and then decided he had better do as his father had said and go to the galley.

Tommy found Cook and Brian, the Galley Boy, sitting at one of the tables in the mess engrossed in a game of draughts. On the side table, under the wall hatch, was a big teapot, a jug of milk, a bowl of sugar and three mugs. Cook spoke,

"Thought you'd got lost, daft lad. Just in time to pour us a cup of tea. It should be mashed by now." Tommy was about to say something, but caught Brian's glance, silently telling him to keep quiet, so he poured the tea. The three of them had a mug of hot steaming tea in front of them and Tommy watched the game in silence wishing he was playing too. Maybe he would be able to play draughts with Brian or Mike at some time during the trip.

When the game of draughts was finished, Cook stood up, placed his hands in the small of his back, stretched and yawned. He spoke to Brian,

"Well, this won't get the jobs done. Come on Brian, go and get me some flour from the store. I've got to make pastry for tonight's meat and tatie pie."

"Anything I can do?" Tommy asked eagerly.

"You can help Brian."

Brian seemed to panic and stuttered, sounding like a deep fog horn,

"No. No. I can manage. Honestly. It's alright."

"Don't be daft. Let the lad help," Cook replied impatiently, turning his back on them and going into the galley.

Brian looked worried as they made their way to the store along the corridor. He opened the door and they stepped in. Tommy's chest felt tight again and, almost immediately, he was gasping for breath. He sat on the floor, took his paper bag out of his pocket and promptly started to blow, in and out, in and out.

Brian came up close to him, took hold of his arm and, obviously worried, whispered hoarsely,

"What's matter? What's matter?"

As Tommy was struggling, he noticed a small cage in the corner on the floor, behind a big box. Puffing and panting into his paper bag, he pointed to the cage and tried to crawl to the door. He had to get out. Brian was really panicking now. He opened the door and helped Tommy out into the corridor where he sat with his back against the wall, the paper bag still around his mouth, hoping no one would see.

"What's matter? What's matter?" Brian pleaded, and he was so scared, his face had turned bright pink.

Still panting, Tommy pointed to the store room. Brian knew he was in trouble, but helped Tommy to his feet and took him to his cabin. Slowly he started to breathe normally again.

"You won't tell will you?" Brian Whimpered, "Promise you won't tell."

"What is it?" Tommy asked.

"It's my pet hamster. I bought it when I got home after the last trip and my mother went crazy. She said she'd chuck it out when I came back to sea." Tommy felt a bit sorry for him.

"I'm allergic to animal fur, but you can't leave it there. If Cook finds it he'll go mad. Can't you

56

have it in your cabin?"

"There's only the cupboard to hide him in and it's dark in there," Brian whined.

"He's better off in the dark than overboard."
Brian thought for a minute,

"Yes, you're right," he admitted glumly. "Will you cover for me while I go and get him?"

"Alright," Tommy replied, "but be quick."
And to think Cook was calling Tommy a daft lad.

Tommy went back into the galley where Cook was cutting some meat on a large block of wood.

"Brian wants to know if you need anything else from the store."

"No, just tell him to get a move on," Cook snapped, "we haven't got all day."

Tommy went back into the passage where Brian grabbed him by the sleeve and dragged him away from the galley. His panic-stricken face whispering,

"He's gone!"

"What do you mean he's gone?" Tommy asked.

"The cage door is open and he's not inside. I don't know where he is."

"He's got to be in there somewhere. Find him before Cook does or you'll be in big trouble," Tommy warned him.

"How much longer are you two going to be?" boomed the Cook from the galley.

"Coming," replied Brian before dashing into the store and coming out with the bin of flour.

Tommy left Brian and Cook in the galley and went out onto the deck where a few of the hands were busy doing their jobs, the Bosun and the Mate giving instructions. The men worked skillfully together, exchanging banter all the time. He went up onto the boat deck to be alone and out of everybody's way.

The Stella Vega was rolling steadily as they proceeded at full steam north towards the fishing grounds. Tommy stood on the deck leaning against the derrick that supported the portside lifeboat with his hands behind his back, listening to the hissing and swishing of the waves as they hit the bows of the ship and he thought about his journey so far. He was sorry he had upset his father, even though he

58

didn't know what he had done wrong, and wondered if he should stay out of his way for the rest of the trip. He also wondered what Brian was going to do about his hamster. He felt sorry for Brian and sorry he wouldn't be able to help him. Stupid asthma!

Tommy was glad of his Guernsey as the wind was quite fresh. He remembered his mother knitting it as she sat in front of the television every night. He felt lonely and thought of home.

Three years ago, just after his father had been made Skipper, they moved from their two up, two down terraced house on West Dock Avenue off Hessle Road, to a semi-detached house on Anlaby Park Road South, a 'posh' area of West Hull. The new house was very different to the one they had left. It was bigger and much quieter. But Tommy frequently thought of his old house. In West Dock Avenue he could often hear the 'clip-clop' of clogs on the pavement outside as the workers made their way down the street and then through the tunnel to the fish dock to work, and then back again when the shift was done. They didn't work regular hours as it all depended on the tides and the trawlers coming in or sailing on that tide. The house walls were thin and you could hear what was happening in your neighbours' houses. When the men were at sea for three weeks it was mostly quiet, but when they came home for their two day break, it was sometimes like all hell had broken loose. The men would collect their wages and then go straight to the pub, and there were a lot of pubs on Hessle Road, the nearest being The Star and Garter, also known as 'Rayners', on the corner of West Dock Avenue and Hessle Road. A favourite haunt for many in the evening was Dee Street Club. That's where his father sometimes took his mother when he was at home. But first he would buy her a new dress to wear. Tommy remembered one particular dress his father had brought home for his mother. It had lots of sequins on it making it shimmer and shine in the light, and Tommy thought she looked like a glamorous singer they sometimes saw on the telly. Tommy missed his old house. There were not many trawler families near the new house. There was another Skipper three doors down, a Mate down Wascana Close and a Radio Operator down Lynton Avenue. The houses in this area were much bigger and more spacious than the terrace they had left behind. Here, they had a front garden, a back garden, a side drive and a garage, even though they didn't have a car. His father would say, "Why spend all that money on a car when there are plenty of buses and taxis?"

All this compared to the house they had left, with the front door opening onto the street and a small yard at the back of the house. It was great playing out in the garden, but he did miss playing out in the street with his old school friends. They would play football, tig or cowboys and Indians, and sometimes annoy the girls who played hopscotch or with skipping ropes that reached right across the street. Children didn't play out in the street in Anlaby Park Road South, not when they had gardens to play in and the Costello Playing Fields and Peter Pan Park just across Boothferry Road. The Costello Playing

Fields were a really big area, with trees and lots of grass where Tommy and his friends would ride their bikes. His mother sometimes took him and his sisters there for a picnic on a Sunday when their father was at sea. Peter Pan Park was at the far end of the playing fields, next to Pickering Road. Tommy loved to go and play on the swings and the slide and sometimes he and his friends would hire a boat on the boating lake and pretend not to hear when the boat-keeper shouted, "Come in number six, your time is up."

What impressed him most about the new house was the upstairs bathroom with a sink, a toilet and a bath with running hot water. There wasn't a bathroom in the old house, just a toilet outside in the back yard and a tin bath hung up on the yard wall which was taken into the house once a week, usually a Friday night. Mother would fill it with hot water from the kettle and, one at a time, the family would 'have a bath'. The rest of the week it was just a strip wash in the back kitchen. That was the past. Now they didn't have to put their coats on in the winter when they had to go out for a wee, and during the night there was now no need to use the potty when the toilet was just across the landing. What luxury!

CHAPTER FIVE

Tommy looked up into the bright, blue sky as he was thinking of home. Seagulls were gliding and screeching overhead, following as though they knew about the fish to be caught in just a few days time.

"Skipper wants you."

Tommy felt sick as he turned to see Norman, the Radio Operator standing by him. Norman put his hand on Tommy's shoulder as they made their way up to the bridge. His father was waiting for him at the wheel and Norman left them alone. Tommy stood with his head down, looking at the floor and his hands behind his back trying to hide his shaking. His father spoke seriously but softly as he said,

"Maybe I shouldn't have shouted at you the way I did, but you have to realize that there are some things we just don't do on board, and whistling is one of them. Do you know why?"

"No, Dad," Tommy mumbled, still looking down

64

at the floor.

"We're a superstitious lot us fishermen, as you already know, and it's said that if you whistle on board you are calling the wind. Not just any wind mind, roaring gales, and we don't want that do we son?"

"No, Dad."

"Well, I'm sure you won't do it again. If you've nothing else to do you can take the wheel again."

Tommy looked up at his father and, seeing the creases around his sparkling eyes, he knew he was forgiven.

"Thanks Dad." He breathed out a great sigh of relief. Phew!

Smiling, he took the wheel once more, glad his father was no longer angry with him, and very glad to be steering the Stella Vega north towards the fishing grounds. In charge again. Captain Tommy Ellis.

That evening, Tommy went to the mess and helped Brian serve the meat and potato pie to the crew, ignoring the comments and digs that were coming his way. Some of the men called him 'spy', some called him 'snivelling kid', and others just ignored him. He recognized Gallagher who had been at the wheel earlier that day. He was sitting next to a man who also had a long nose, pointed chin and steely eyes, so Tommy imagined it was his brother. They talked quietly together, now and again looking up at Tommy. Once the meal was over, he and Brian cleared everything away and washed the dishes, chatting all the time. Brian talked of his father who was Bosun on another trawler, and his elder brother who, like him, had started as Galley Boy, then went on to be a Deckie Learner, and was at that moment in time working as a spare hand. He said his brother was ambitious and wanted to take all his tickets and eventually become a Skipper.

"Do you want to be a Skipper one day?" Tommy asked him.

"No, not me. I'd rather work in the galley where it's warm. I think I'll be a Cook."

As they were finishing, Tommy checked that no

one else was around and whispered to Brian,

"Have you found the hamster yet?"

"No, I haven't had chance to look. I'll wait until everybody's settled down, then I'll go and look. Will you come and help me?"

"I wish I could," Tommy replied apologetically, "but I told you I'm allergic to animal fur. I hope you find him before Cook does."

Brian's face turned very pale as he said,

"So do I."

Tommy went to bed at the same time as everybody else. Mike, who was sharing his cabin with him, rambled on for a while about the work he had to do the next day, but soon fell asleep. Maybe it was the uncomfortable bunk he was lying in, or maybe it was the continuous roll of the ship and the beating, vibrating rhythm of the engines, but Tommy couldn't sleep. He got out of bed, quietly picked up his trousers, guernsey and boots, and crept outside into the passageway, trying not to wake Mike. The cabin door wasn't closed, but left ajar so that they could get some fresh air, therefore making it easy for him to sneak out. The lights were still on in the passage so it wasn't difficult to find his way to the deck. He looked at his watch and saw it was just gone midnight.

Outside he saw the most amazing, breathtaking sight he had ever seen. Millions and millions of stars, all shining so very brightly against a black sky. Some were bigger than others and twinkling more than others. He had seen starry nights back home in Hull, but nothing to compare to this. He recognized the Milky Way, stretched out like a ribbon, from one side of the sky to the other. He'd heard of the Polar Star and wondered which one it was. He knew one of those stars was the Stella Vega, but which one? His neck started to ache, so he decided to lie down on the deck and look upwards. As he was looking for somewhere to lie down, he noticed a movement further along the deck towards the fo'c'sle. He ducked down behind the winch, scared he would be seen. He heard whispering, but couldn't understand what was being said. Whoever it was, they were moving something about. Then he felt the vibration of footsteps as they came closer to the bridge. Tommy held his breath as he stood in the dark shadow between the bridge and the winch, and, eyes open wide, he watched as the Gallagher brothers walked by and went inside. Phew, they hadn't seen him. When he felt it was safe to move again, he crept towards the doorway, opened it just enough to get a clear view of the passage, saw it was clear, darted inside and back to his cabin. He fumbled to get undressed and back into his bunk trying not to disturb Mike's snoring. What was he going to do? Should he tell somebody what he had seen? But, what had he seen? With these questions pounding in his head over and over again, Tommy fell asleep.

CHAPTER SIX

"Are you going to stay there all day, daft lad?"
Tommy opened his eyes to be greeted by the sight
of Cook standing in the doorway, hands on hips.
He nearly banged his head on the shelf above as he
hastily sat up, turning to jump out of his bunk.

"Get a move on. It's gone six," Cooked growled
before he went away.

Tommy looked around. Mike's bunk was empty,
so he jumped out of bed, found his trousers and
guernsey where he had left them at the bottom of
his bunk the night before, and got dressed. He
remembered what he had seen and still hadn't
decided whether or not to tell anyone. If he told his
father, that would be telling tales. He had to tell
someone, but who? Who could he trust? He knew
Brian's secret and Mike had told him to watch out
for the Gallagher brothers. But maybe it was
nothing at all. Maybe they were just out on deck
looking at the stars as he was. He decided he would

say nothing, but that night he would go out on deck again. He wanted to find out if there was anything going on, and if there was, what was it? He quickly splashed his face with water and tried to plaster down his sticky-up hair, then went to work.

Tommy laid the tables in the mess and made a big pot of tea ready for breakfast at seven o'clock. Most of the crew tucked into their plates piled high with bacon, sausage, eggs and beans, dipping doorsteps of bread and butter into the eggs and beans. All was washed down with hot, steaming tea.

"You do make a good cup of tea, lad, I'll give you that," said one of the men to Tommy, "keep it up." Tommy smiled back at him thinking, 'I should be alright if I carry on like this.'

The Gallagher brothers were eating their breakfast in the far corner of the mess, and Tommy kept glancing at them. Mike saw who Tommy was looking at and caught him later in the passage saying,

"They're up to something those two. Wish I

71

knew what it was."

Tommy couldn't say anything there and then as there were too many people about, but decided he would tell Mike about what he had seen and get him to go out on deck with him that night.

After breakfast he asked Brian,

"Any luck with the hamster?"

"No," Brian whispered, "I can't find it anywhere. I'll try again later."

Tommy hoped he would find it soon and keep it locked away. What if Cook went into that storeroom and saw a hamster running loose? At the thought of Cook seeing the hamster, an icy cold shiver ran down the whole length of Tommy's spine Once everything had been cleared away after breakfast, Tommy went up onto the bridge where one of the Gallagher brothers was at the wheel. He said 'Hello', but only got a grunt for a reply.

Looking out of the window he saw that it was pouring with rain. Down on the deck, the men who were working wore oilskin frocks and sou'westers, and they looked drenched.   He was glad to be inside where it was dry. He had heard about the harsh weather conditions in the Arctic during the winter months, but he had no idea of how severe it really was. He tried to imagine the crew working hard to chip ice off the structure of the ship, which, he had been told, could make the ship top-heavy and turn over, sending it to the bottom of the sea, something that happened nearly every winter. But this was summer time, and, even so, as they were sailing further north, he had felt a drop in the temperature.

In his geography lessons at school he had learned about the midnight sun up in the Arctic and how it was still daylight at eleven o'clock at night. He had also learnt that during the winter months it was dark most of the time, so he was glad he was going up there in the summer. He didn't like the long nights in winter when it was dark when he went to school in the morning, and it was dark again when he left school at four o'clock to go home. He thought it must be awful to live in the dark all day long.

"If you've nothing better to do, you can go and

help Deckie," his father said as he came out of the chart room.

"He's in the fo'c'sle. I'll tell Bosun you're on your way. Go and get your waterproof gear on."

With his boots up to the top of his thighs, his oilskin frock down below his knees and his sou'wester nearly covering his eyes, Tommy went out into the driving rain. The deck was very slippery so he had to hold on to whatever he could to steady himself with the roll of the ship. He wasn't wearing gloves and the cold wet metal seemed to cut into his hands. He entered the fo'c'sle and fell into a heap as he tripped over something that was lying on the floor. Mike laughed,

"You look like a drowned rat."

Tommy laughed too,

"I feel like one. I've been sent to give you a hand."

He looked around at the metal walls that sloped down from the ceiling and from a point towards the front. They were right at the front end of the ship where the waves hit first. There was a loud thump and a massive shudder each time they hit a wave. He had been told that in the older trawlers, the crew had to sleep in there, in the fo'c'sle. It must have been horribly noisy and cold.

Mike told him to take his wet frock off first, then, showed him how to repair nets. As they worked, Tommy decided it would be a good time to tell him about the Gallagher brothers. He explained what had happened the night before and asked Mike if he would go out with him that night to see if they were there again.

"Have you told anybody else? Brian, the Galley Boy?" Mike asked.

"No," Tommy replied, "only you."

"I knew they were up to something," Mike said nodding his head. "We'll have to be very careful though. I've already told you the Gallagher brothers are a rough lot. I don't trust them. In the meantime, don't tell anybody else. Not until we know for sure what they're up to."

Tommy understood what Mike was saying. He

75

would act like nothing had happened.

It poured with rain for the rest of that day. Tommy helped Mike with the nets between helping Cook and Brian in the galley. That night they had minced beef, onions, mashed potatoes and peas for tea. There was plenty of it and, as Tommy had recovered from his seasickness, he tucked in and really enjoyed it.

As the evening wore on, the ship started to roll more than it had done during the day. Tommy, Mike, Brian and one of the spare hands were playing dominoes in the mess. Brian was fidgeting the whole time and Tommy couldn't wait to ask him if he'd found his hamster. The Mate put his head into the mess doorway,

"Check everything's lashed down. We're in for some bad weather." Then he was gone.

No one hesitated, not even for a second. Card games, draughts and dominoes were abandoned as the men, including Mike, jumped up and left the mess.

"What do we do?" Tommy asked Brian.

"Nothing much. Let's clear up here though."

Once all the playing cards were back in their packets and the draughts and dominoes in their boxes, Tommy asked Brian if he had found the hamster.

"Not yet. I'll go now whilst everybody's busy."

Tommy left Brian and went up on the bridge. The ship was rolling heavily and he had to hold on to the hand rails as he walked along the passageways to stop himself from being thrown from one side to the other.

Up on the bridge, the bosun was at the wheel and Tommy's father was looking out of the window. It was dark outside, but big floodlights had been switched on, illuminating the whole deck. The rigging was pinging against the masts and the derricks as the wind whistled through. All the men were dressed in their oilskins and were staggering around, bending into the wind, making sure nothing was loose, while waves continually lashed the deck. The bows heaved up to the top of the waves, and plunged down into the darkness, again and again, pitching and rolling, thrashing through the black swell of the sea.

Tommy was feeling queasy and tasted his minced beef and onions again. He turned to his father to tell him he was going below. However, he noticed that his father didn't look very well and was burping while holding his hand over his mouth. He managed to say,

"I'm going down."

His father was just able to manage a nod in reply.

Tommy went straight to the crew toilet area and was sick. He managed to get back to his cabin and wasn't there long before Mike came staggering in mumbling,

"Don't know what's the matter with everybody, they're all being sick, me as well. Good job the waves are coming over to clean the deck."

"Is it because of the bad weather?" Tommy asked.

"Don't think so. First day out maybe, but not now. These blokes are used to it after all the years they've been going to sea," Mike replied before putting his hand over his mouth and scarpering out of the cabin.

Tommy lay in his bunk on his side, hanging on to the rail to stop himself from being tossed about. He had a splitting headache and he felt dizzy, but he did manage to get off to sleep. Mike came back to the cabin and woke him saying,

"We won't be able to go out and watch the Gallagher brothers tonight in this weather. It's too dangerous. We'll do it tomorrow."

Tommy had forgotten about the Gallagher brothers. He knew that Mike was right so he closed his eyes and went back to sleep.

CHAPTER SEVEN

The seasickness had only lasted one night, but the bad weather continued for another two days. They had gone beyond the Arctic Circle and were exactly where the cold, dark blue current from the Polar regions was coming down from the Barents Sea and meeting up and clashing with the warmer, brown coloured North Atlantic Current, waves meeting and rising, breaking into foam as though they were fighting, each trying its best to push the other away. Tommy helped a lot in the galley and Cook still called him a 'daft lad'.   Working in the galley in heavy seas was dangerous.   Whatever was cooking sloshed around in the pans with the movement of the ship. Tommy now understood why Cook had so many scars on his forearms. They were burns and scalds.

He liked Brian, always wearing the same grubby looking apron, but felt sorry for him as he couldn't find his hamster and was worried somebody else might find it. Tommy hadn't had any more asthma attacks, so it couldn't be where it was before. He wished he could have helped find it, but the last thing he wanted was another attack, especially in front of the crew. Poor Brian.

The crew couldn't do much work on deck in the bad weather, so they hung around the mess playing card games or dominoes. Some just stayed in their cabins and read magazines. The Gallagher brothers were always together and didn't seem to mix with any of their shipmates. At least, Tommy thought, they wouldn't have been able to go out on deck at night time again.

Tommy went up to the wheelhouse as often as he could. He stood for ages looking out of the window at the sea. Some of the waves were as big as houses and the bows of the ship slowly pushed up to the top, struggling and groaning, then thrust down into the valley below getting ready to attack the next wave. Even inside the bridge he could hear the howling wind and people had to shout to make themselves heard above the noise. The whole ship shuddered violently as each wave hit and everybody had to hold on so as not to fall over.

He sometimes went into the chart room and the radio room. He liked the radio room and was fascinated by all the equipment in there. Norman, the Radio Operator, was a nice man and explained some of the equipment to him. Norman was often busy sending or receiving messages in morse code, which for Tommy just sounded like 'da di da di da.' There were also quite a few log books where Norman would regularly enter sets of figures. Tommy asked what the figures were and Norman told him they were records of their position, the atmospheric pressure and the weather. He said that all the Hull Trawlers kept these records as they were useful to measure all the changes that happened and could be used for future trips. Tommy had studied things like that in his geography lessons at school and often wondered what use they were. Now he knew and was fascinated.

"What's this book for?" Tommy asked, noticing a

green coloured log book which lay open showing numbers and nationalities of ships.

"Nothing," stammered Norman, nervously.

He stood up and closed the green book. Trying to sound more cheerful he added,

"We just like to keep a check on how many different nationalities fish around here. We keep it to ourselves though as we don't want others to think we're spying on them." He winked at Tommy.

Tommy was confused, but didn't ask any more questions as Norman had turned away from him, put his headphones on and started to tune in his radio.

The storm seemed to end suddenly. The sea was still a bit rough and the ship was rolling, but not as much as before. It stayed that way for the whole of that day.

"Stand by!" Was heard throughout the ship in the early hours of the next morning.

Tommy was startled. What was happening? What was he supposed to do? He went to the galley where Cook was bobbing about getting this and moving that in anticipation that something very important was going to happen.

"From now on daft lad, it's your job to make sure the teapot in the mess is always full and the tea is hot. Have you got that?"

"Yes," was the sharp answer.

"And make sure the Skipper has plenty of tea, sugar and milk up on the bridge."

"Yes, Cook," Tommy felt like stamping his feet, clicking his heels, saluting and shouting, "Yes Sergeant Major!"

First, Tommy made a large pot of tea for the mess, then he took two packets of tea, a bag of sugar and a bottle of milk up to the bridge.

It had just turned daylight and the crew, wearing their oilskin frocks, sou'westers and sea boots, were busying themselves on the deck getting the trawl ready to shoot.   Everybody was moving very quickly, each man knowing exactly where he should be and what he should be doing.   The ship's telegraph sounded giving a signal to the chief engineer to slow the engines.   Shooting the trawl

84

looked to be very dangerous. There were ropes, chains and thick wire cables along the deck and the crew moved around mindful of the dangers that surrounded them. The net was enormous. It had a smaller section at the bottom called the 'cod end' which was where the fish would go as they trawled the sea bed. The cod end was covered with cow hides which were there to protect it from snagging on the rocks or anything else which could be on the bottom, like a sunken ship for example. The opening of the net was very wide and had a large wooden board, an 'otter board', attached to each side to keep it open whilst trawling. The bottom of the net was attached to very large bobbins that would roll along the sea bed. The net was cast over the starboard side of the ship.

All the time, Tommy's father was observing from the bridge window. The Mate was in charge on deck.

"Are we fishing now, Dad?" Tommy was excited.

"Hello son. Didn't see you there. Yes we are. You just stand over at yon side of the bridge so you can see what's going on."

Tommy did as he was told and asked,

"How long will it take?"

"A while."

"Do the men stay there to wait until it's ready to pull in?"

"No lad. We're going to split the men into three shifts now. Eighteen hours on and six off. That will go on all the time we're fishing. It'll be hard for the third shift as they will have been on deck working for about thirty six hours before they get their turn for a rest, apart from when they can go and get something to eat. Some of the crew will be below deck to store the fish in the ice pounds."

"And how long do we fish for?"

"Eight or nine days, depends on how much we catch."

Tommy looked out of the window again and noticed that one of the hatches was open and planks of wood were being lifted out and fitted into slots on the deck. The deck hands were making pounds, square sections on the deck where the fish would be dropped and stopped from rolling back into the sea after they had been released from the cod end.

Tommy remembered what Cook had told him to do, so he left the bridge and went to check the tea in the mess. Just in time. The tea pot was nearly empty and cook was nowhere to be seen. As he finished, some of the crew came in, one saying,

"Just what we need. Thanks lad."

Tommy smiled back at them. It seemed that a few of the crew members were starting to accept him. He must remember to keep an eye on that teapot or he'd be in trouble, and not only from the cook. He made sure there were plenty of clean mugs, milk and sugar, and took the dirty mugs to the galley to wash. Cook came back barking another order,

"Glad you're here. Go and get me a bin of flour."

"Where is it?"

"In the store."

That was where the hamster had been. What was he going to do? He checked his pocket to see if he had remembered his paper bag. It was there, so he made his way to the store. Tommy hesitated at first, and taking a deep breath, stepped in. Nothing. No tight chest and no wheezing. Brian must have found his hamster and hidden it somewhere else, but as he stepped out of the store, his eyes noticed something to the left. There it was. Brian's hamster scuttling down the passage along the wall. Tommy held his breath as he watched it climb over a ledge and into Cook's cabin. He had to find Brian and tell him straight away. Of all the places for it to go. Cook's cabin!

Trying to act as though nothing had happened, he asked Cook,

"Where's Brian?"

"Cleaning the toilets. Why? Do you want to help him daft lad?"

Tommy glared back at him,

"No, I just wondered." He turned and left the galley.

"Brian, Brian," Tommy said quietly, looking round to see if anyone else was nearby. "It's in Cook's cabin."

Brian glanced back at him vacantly, not quite

88

understanding what he'd said. Tommy repeated urgently,

"It's in Cook's cabin. I've just seen your hamster go into Cook's cabin."

Brian's face turned pale.

"Are you sure?"

"Am I sure? 'course I'm sure. I saw it with my own eyes. It went into Cook's cabin. Anyway, I've got to go now." Tommy looked around again and scuttled away.

Tommy checked the tea pot again before going back to the bridge. As he moved forward, he began to hear loud noises. The noises were the voices of the crew shouting to each other as they worked, the sound of metal banging against metal, chains clanking, and the chug, chug of the winch motor. To his horror he felt the ship list to one side. His heart began to pound rapidly and loudly in his chest as he thought, 'We're going over! We're going over!'

Panicking, he ran up to the bridge where his father was still in his usual place, looking tense, but at the same time, calm. He had a mug of tea in his hand and lowered his head slightly to take a sip. Tommy looked out of the window and saw the reason for the list. The net was being hauled in over the starboard side and the weight of it, being full of fish, was pulling on the ship. The deck hands were in a line along the side and, as each wave came towards them, they lifted the net, in unison heaving the next section on board. Tommy could see why they needed the oilskin frocks. They were wide and long, coming to below their knees and over their boots. Being made of oilskin, they would not only keep them dry, but would also protect them from the wind.

When the wave rose towards them, all the men steadied themselves on the wet, slippery deck while they hung over the side and pulled in the net. All the while, the Mate and the Bosun were shouting orders which no one hesitated to obey. This was dangerous work and Tommy had already heard tales of men being lost overboard. He peered down over the deck and saw Mike moving towards the winch which was situated just below the bridge. The motor kicked in and he saw how the thick cables and chains became taught as they began to haul the net upwards out of the water. The voluminous cod end was floating on the surface and there were what seemed to be hundreds of sea birds screeching and swooping down over the fish in the net. Slowly the net was lifted out of the water and swung over the deck, dripping heavily, the wet cow hides flapping around the bottom. Once it was over the pounds, the Mate moved forward to release the cod rope at the bottom of the bulging net and, as he pulled it, the contents gushed out and he jumped out of the way fast. As soon as the net was empty, it was quickly checked for damage and, because it hadn't been damaged, the cod rope was tied again and the gear was prepared for the next shoot.

The deck hands picked up the fish in one hand and with the other, deftly used their knives to remove the innards. The fish, bigger than any Tommy had ever seen before, some as big as a man's arm, thrashed as their red livers were yanked out and thrown into a nearby bin. The rest of the innards were tossed over the side of the ship and the fish was then thrown into the washer, a tank in the middle of the deck, and from there it would go down into the hold to be stored on ice. Every man was working as fast as he possibly could. The smell of fish was already seeping through to the bridge.

"What sort of fish is it, Dad?" Tommy asked.

"Cod, son."

Tommy spent that first day's fishing between the bridge, the mess and the galley. His father let him take the wheel a few times when they were trawling the net, but not when they were shooting or hauling. When he was at the wheel he was Captain Tommy again, head held high and proud, just like the pirate captains he had seen in films.

There was fish for dinner and fish for tea, and Cook told him it would be fish for breakfast too, every day while they were hauling them in. Tommy liked fish and chips, but they only had it once a week at home. He thought about the queues outside Ed Fletcher's fish shop on Hessle Road. People said it was the best fish shop in Hull. But as he was going to have fish for breakfast, dinner and tea every day here, would he still want fish and chips when he got home? Maybe not.

CHAPTER EIGHT

The crew worked their eighteen hour shifts all through the night and into the next day. In the afternoon, the net came up damaged, so it had to be changed and the damaged one repaired. It happened during Mike's shift, so, once the new net had gone over the side and they were trawling, Tommy was told to help Mike in the fo'c'sle.

Feeling very pleased that at last he was going down to join the fishermen, he put on his sea boots and oil skin frock and went out on deck to make his way forward along the port side of the ship where no one was working, so as to keep out of everybody's way. This was the first time he had been out on deck since the fishing had started. As the ship was heaving its way up to the crest of the wave, Tommy, with arms outstretched, steadied himself, then, slipping and sliding, he was skating down the deck, following the ship into the dip between the waves. He was enjoying this, it was

94

great fun, just like sliding on the ice along the pavements during the winter at home, but suddenly, a voice screamed out,

"Water!"

Tommy felt as though he had been hit by an express train as someone grabbed hold of him and held him down as they were battered by a huge wall of water. Whoever it was didn't let go and stayed with him until the water had gushed out of the portholes back into the sea. Coughing and spluttering, he looked up and saw it was one of the Gallaghers who was now helping him to his feet and saying,

"That was close."

His father was soon by his side.

"I thought we'd lost you," his father's voice was urgent and hoarse.

"I'm alright Dad. What happened?" Tommy couldn't control his shaking. It was as though something like that had happened to him before, but he couldn't remember when.

"It was a rogue wave. We get them sometimes

when the sea's a bit rough. Whoever sees it coming shouts, 'Water', and everybody grabs hold of something, a hand rail or something. I should have told you about rogue waves. I'm sorry son. If it wasn't for Sid Gallagher, you'd have gone over. He was certainly quick off the mark."

Tommy turned round to see Gallagher had gone back to gutting the fish as though nothing had happened at all.

Tommy stayed inside for the rest of that day checking the teapot and making sure there were plenty of clean cups, milk and sugar for the men when they came in. By tea time he was feeling quite hungry so, he went to the mess to eat with the others. There were mutterings and people staring at him. The Cook said,

"You were very lucky you know. You could have gone over the side."

Someone else butted in saying,

"Lucky? That wasn't luck. If it hadn't been for Sid Gallagher he would have been a gonner."

Tommy, feeling very sheepish, asked,

"Where is Mr. Gallagher? I want to thank him."

"In his cabin," was the abrupt reply.

Tommy made his way aft and came across a four berth cabin. He knocked on the half-open door and someone answered,

"Come in."

Sid Gallagher was lying in his bunk and his brother was sitting on another bunk opposite him.

"What do you want?"

"I've come to say thank you for helping me," Tommy stammered.

"The deck is no place for a kid, especially in this weather," Sid's brother said, shaking his head.

"I was going to help Mike mend the nets."

"I know. But you should have been holding on to the hand rail.

"I'm sorry."

"No need to be sorry. If you go out there again, hold on."

"I will," Tommy replied, hoping he wouldn't have to go out on deck again in bad weather.

"Are you ready for something to eat?" he continued

97

trying to sound friendly "There's plenty."

"Yeah. See ya." Tommy was dismissed without ceremony.

Tommy returned to the mess feeling embarrassed and ashamed. Ashamed at being stupid enough not to think of holding on. Stupid enough not to recognize the dangers. He didn't look at or speak to anyone as he checked the teapot and collected the dirty dishes. The Cook didn't say anything to him either as he did the washing up. Tommy was glad for the silence. He felt it was an apt punishment. Head held low and hunched shoulders, he carried on until he had finished washing the dishes and everything was dried and put away.

CHAPTER NINE

The fishing continued that night and the next day and no one spoke of Tommy's incident. Everyone just carried on as though nothing had happened. The Country and Western music still played over the loud speaker with some people singing along to the well-known songs. The crew carried on with their eighteen hours on, six hours off shifts, all through the day and night. The skipper never left the bridge, except for a couple of hours sleep on the sofa in the chart room while the net was out.

There was plenty of fish to fry in the galley. As Cook had said, fish for breakfast, fish for dinner and fish for tea. There was even cold fish to make sandwiches for supper. Tommy made sure the teapot was always full, he washed dishes, peeled potatoes and went up on to the bridge.

Tommy was allowed to take the wheel for short periods of time and he also went into the radio room to watch Norman. He was on the bridge after dark, watching the deck hands gutting the fish under the floodlights when he heard the Radio Operator talking to someone. The conversation ended with Norman saying,

"Cheers Eric. Over and out," then, seeing Tommy in the doorway said,

"Come in, I'll show you something." Pointing to a large screen over in the corner. It was a dark screen with some green marks on it and a line that moved round the radius clockwise, sending out a 'bleep' sound as it crossed another green mark. Norman pointed to some of the green marks close to the centre and said,

"These marks are other trawlers. Some of them are from Hull, some from Grimsby and some are from other countries. Now these marks here, near the outside edge of the screen, are icebergs. I've just been on the air with the Radio Operator of the Stella Antares and they've spotted one."

Tommy was fascinated.

"Icebergs?" he asked, surprised as he didn't expect icebergs in summer.

"Yes, big chunks of ice that have broken off the glaciers at either Franz Joseph Island or Spitzbergen. They drift south on the strong currents."

"Are they dangerous?"

"They can be. We've got to be careful not to get too close."

"But it's dark outside. We can't see them. How do we look out for them?" Tommy asked.

"We keep an eye on the radar."

Tommy went onto the bridge to look out of the window, but all was black beyond the glaring lights on deck.

"What are you looking for?" his father asked.

"Icebergs," replied Tommy intently.

"Well, let me know if you see one," his father chuckled.

On his way to bed that night, Tommy passed by the Cook's cabin and the door was open. His chest became tight and he started to wheeze. He had completely forgotten about Brian's hamster and realized it was still in Cook's cabin. He didn't have

101

his paper bag with him but he managed to struggle to his own cabin to get one from under his mattress. He slid down to the floor and breathed in and out, in and out.

"What are you doing?"

He hadn't noticed Mike asleep in his bunk.

He took the bag away for a second to gasp,

"Asthma," then continued to inflate and deflate the paper bag again.

Worried, Mike looked on but waited until Tommy's breathing was easier before speaking again.

"What's brought that on?"

Tommy didn't know what to do. Should he tell Mike about Brian's hamster? If he didn't, how was he going to explain his asthma? What would Brian say? Mike was nice and Tommy was sure he could be trusted.

He was about to speak when they heard a roar and a clatter coming from further down the passageway. Both boys jumped up and went to the door.

"It was in my bed! The blooming thing was in my bed!" Cook yelled as he ran up and down the passage way with a shoe in his hand, ready to hit out.

"What's matter Cook?" Mike asked.

"It was in my blooming bed!" Cook snapped back at him.

"Do you know anything about this?" He growled at Mike. Then turning to Tommy he said,

"I bet it was you, daft lad."

Tommy had had enough.

"It wasn't me, and you can stop calling me daft lad. I'm not a daft lad, so stop it!" he yelled back at Cook.

Cook couldn't believe his ears. He had never been spoken to like that before. Not even his galley boys had ever spoken to him like that, and here was this skinny little kid. How dare he?

"Right. That's it. I'm going to see the Skipper," he said indignantly before storming off.

"What was all that about?" Mike asked.

"Brian's hamster."

"Brian's what?"

"His hamster. He brought it on board with him.

He hid it in the stores first and then it got away. That's why I get asthma. I'm allergic to animal fur," Tommy explained.

"There's going to be trouble now. We'd better warn Brian."

When they found Brian and told him what had happened, he turned on Tommy.

"I thought I could trust you, but no. Off you go telling tales. You're just like all the rest of them."

"I didn't tell. Honest," Tommy pleaded. "He found it in his bed, didn't he Mike?"

"You're rotten you are," Brian barked in his deep croaky voice before running off.

Tommy started to go after him but Mike took hold of his arm.

"Don't worry about it," Mike said. "He'll get over it. He'll have to."

"But Cook doesn't know it was Brian's. He thinks I put it there," Tommy said, overwhelmed by what had just happened.

"I wonder where it is now. Poor little thing just scooted aft towards the bathrooms," Mike said.

104

"I should go and see my Dad. Heaven knows what sort of a story Cook is telling him."

"I'll come with you."

Tommy and Mike went up to the bridge where they found Cook still ranting and raving. The Skipper was scratching his head and saying,

"You mean to tell me that my lad put a mouse in your bed?"

"That's right Skipper. The crafty little beggar must have thought it was some kind of a joke. But I don't think it's funny. Frightened the living daylights out of me it did."

"Well, I can tell you one thing for sure and that is, it wasn't my lad."

"'Course it was him. Who else could it have been?" returned the Cook indignantly.

"I know it wasn't him because he's allergic to animal fur. Can't go anywhere near them."

The Cook took a step back, not believing what he was hearing. He turned round and stormed off the bridge saying between his teeth,

"I'll get to the bottom of this if it's the last thing I

do." and he was gone.

The Skipper turned to Tommy and Mike trying to keep a straight face,

"Well, out with it, what's going on?"

Mike spoke first,

"I didn't know anything about it until Cook came storming out of his cabin, honest Skipper."

Tommy's Dad thought for a moment before saying,

"I believe you. I've known you and your family for years and it's not the sort of prank you would pull off. Go and get some sleep. Your shift starts in a couple of hours."

Tommy was about to leave with Mike but his father said,

"Not so fast young man. You can stay here and tell me everything you know."

Tommy didn't tell on Brian. He just told his father he knew there was an animal on board because of his asthma attacks, and nothing more. He knew Brian must have been terribly worried and he didn't want to make matters worse for him.

CHAPTER TEN

The next morning, as well as fish for breakfast, there was porridge. A lot of the crew were glad of the change and filled their bowls from the big pan, some adding sugar and some adding salt. Tommy didn't want porridge, so had fish again and so did Mike.

Brian was making himself as scarce as he possibly could. He was very cross with Tommy and didn't speak to him at all the few times they saw each other in the galley or in the mess. Tommy tried to let him know that he hadn't told, but Brian would have nothing of it. Every time Tommy approached him he just lifted his freckled nose in the air and walked away.

Cook was also giving Tommy the cold treatment by muttering instructions to him only when he needed to. Now and then he looked at him, squinting his eyes and nodding his head as if to say, 'I'll get you for this.'

After breakfast, Tommy went up onto the bridge. His father let him steer again for a while and use the binoculars to look out for ice-bergs. By mid-morning, quite a few members of the crew kept running to the toilet, and that included the Skipper and the Radio Operator.

When lunch time came, nobody went to the mess. The Mate came into the galley and said most of the crew were in their bunks with belly ache, and that was where he was going too.

Cook took off his apron and threw it down on the table,

"All that fish cooked for nothing."

Turning to Brian he said,

"Put it in the cold store. I'm not going to waste it." Turning to glare at Tommy he continued,

"You do as you please. Nothing for you to do down here for now. Come back at four o'clock."

Feeling a bit crushed, Tommy left the galley to go back up to the bridge. On his way he met Mike who was coming to find him.

"Come quick," he panted. "Skipper's taken bad

like everybody else."

They both ran as quickly as they could and found the Skipper hanging on to the wheel with one hand, the other holding tight round his middle.

"You'll – have – to – take – the – wheel," he struggled to say, and staggered to his cabin, holding onto the wall as he went.

Tommy and Mike looked at each other. Tommy grabbed the wheel and checked their direction. Mike checked the Radio Room.

"Norman's not there. He must be badly too. Look Tommy, we're going to have to manage. I'll go down on deck and see what's happening there."

Tommy liked taking the wheel when his father was in charge, but it wasn't good up here on his own. What if he did something wrong? He looked down on to the deck and saw Mike talking to the Gallagher brothers. All three looked up to the bridge where Tommy was steering the ship and then started talking again. They didn't talk for very long though before they split up, the Gallaghers staying on deck and going over to the starboard side. Mike came dashing back onto the bridge, panting,

"There's only us, Cook, Brian and the second engineer. We're going to haul the gear in, fish or no fish. We can always shoot again when everybody's better. Sid said just keep her as steady as you can and watch out for his signals."

"What signals?" asked Tommy.

"Hand signals to steer to starboard or port or to slow down. You'll need to turn the ship when the net's coming up, and use that lever over there to tell the engineer when to slow down." He was gone as quickly as he came.

Tommy heard the winch motor turning and saw the cables becoming taught. The Gallaghers were looking over the side and signalling with their arms to Mike, who was operating the winch. Tommy kept his eye on the compass as well as on the Gallaghers. His jaw was aching as he clenched his teeth together. He was now responsible for the whole ship. Looking down, he saw that Cook and Brian had gone out to help. Stan Gallagher looked up at the bridge and turned his arm in the direction he wanted Tommy to turn the wheel. Steadily, Tommy slipped the wheel through his hands, turning the ship starboard, until Stan held up his hand to tell him to hold it where it was. He then signalled for Tommy to turn the wheel to the port side, and then again to hold it. The next signal was to slow down, so he reached over to the lever and pulled it back into the slow position, hoping the engineer was on standby waiting for the signal. Tommy responded immediately and confidently to all Stan Gallagher's signals.

The net came to the surface out of the deep, dark green waters. There were not as many fish as there had been on previous hauls, but they had to get them in just the same. The Gallaghers, Cook and Brian hung over the side and, as the wave rose to lift the net, all moving together, they hauled as much as they could on board. With just the four of them they could only haul in a bit at a time, their muscles tight and strained with the weight of the net. Tommy watched as they were puffing and blowing, their faces strained, trying to breathe in and out as they worked. With the next wave they hauled again and then again, until the cod end was all that was left. Mike set the winch in motion and the cables lifted this last section of net over the deck. One of the Gallaghers jumped forward to release the cod rope, allowing the fish to escape. Cook and Brian set about gutting the fish while Sid and Stan Gallagher dealt with putting away and securing the gear.

Tommy felt very lonely up on the bridge as he watched these experienced fishermen at work. His arms ached terribly, but he didn't dare let go of the wheel. While they had been hauling in the net, Tommy heard the di-di-da of morse code coming through in the radio room, as well as some scratchy, crackling sounds on the radio, but he didn't dare leave the wheel to go and have a look. He looked at the compass and realized they were not sailing in the same direction as before. He remembered he had to change course so as to haul in the net. What should he do now? Stay on the course they were on, or turn the wheel to the direction they were sailing in before? Sid Gallagher appeared on the bridge.

"You did a grand job there Tommy. I'll take over now for a bit."

"I had to turn the wheel when we were hauling, do we go back on the same course as before?" Tommy asked.

"I'll check the chart first," he replied looking at the compass, before going into the chart room. After a short while, Sid Gallagher came back saying,

"If we stay on this course we'll end up in Russia. You go down for something to eat and a cup of tea. I'll sort everything out up here."

This man had saved him from going overboard only a few days before and he was being very nice to him now, but there was something Tommy didn't like about him. Why had he and his brother been out on deck that first night? He didn't trust the Gallagher brothers.

"Alright, see you later. Oh, do you want anything to eat?" Tommy asked.

"Not now thanks," was the curt reply.

Tommy went to his father's cabin to see how he was doing. He found him in his bunk looking very pale and sweaty.

"How are you Dad?" he asked softly.

"My stomach feels as though it's being ripped right out of me. Can you get me some water please? I'm ever-so thirsty."

Tommy found a glass and filled it with water from the tap in the Skipper's bathroom, and his father drank it all in one go, passing the glass back to him to be filled again. After drinking the second glass he asked,

"What's happening?"

"Nearly everybody's poorly, Dad. There's only me, Mike, Cook, Brian, the Gallagher brothers and the Second Engineer that are alright. We've hauled in the net and Sid Gallagher's on watch at the wheel right now."

Tommy's father started to say,

"But how did you...." and was sick again in the bucket by his bunk.

114

Tommy filled the glass with water again and, telling his father to rest, said he would be back later. He wanted to tell his father that he had steered on his own, but decided he would wait until he was better. Next, he went to see Norman and found him in the same state his father was in. It was the same in nearly all the other cabins and Mike, Brian and Tommy spent the rest of the day running backwards and forwards fetching water.

That night, The Gallaghers were on watch on the bridge and Tommy went out on deck for some fresh air. The sea was much calmer and, once again, the sky was full of the most brilliant stars, but what was that smell? It smelt like mould, could it be the fish below deck? And he could hear waves lapping, like at the seaside. Strange. He hadn't heard that before. It was different to the way waves lap up against the ship. He strolled further along the deck towards the fo'c'sle and had a feeling that something wasn't quite right. What was that awful smell? Then he saw it. His eyes nearly popped out of his head at the sight of the huge monster. What appeared to be only a few yards ahead to the port side was an enormous white mountain, much, much bigger than the Stella Vega. An Ice-berg! He shouted as loud as he could, at the top of his voice,

"Ice-berg! Ice-berg!" as he ran inside and up to the bridge. Both Gallaghers looked up as Tommy hurtled in shouting and pointing in the direction of the great beast they were in danger of colliding with. Sid swung the wheel to starboard as Stan hurriedly moved the lever to signal 'Full Astern' to the engine room. At first the ship didn't seem to move, then, slowly she began to swing to the right as the changing engines made the whole ship shudder. Mike, Cook and Brian came flying up to the bridge to see what was happening, and just stood there with their mouths gaping wide as they were sailing past the ice-berg, only a few yards away.

Tommy's father, looking very weak and steadying himself in the doorway came to see what was going on and when he saw their faces he turned to see the ice-berg slowly moving away from them. His chin seemed to sink into his chest as he growled,

"How on earth did that happen?"

"It was Tommy who spotted it Skipper," Sid Gallagher stammered.

The Skipper was angry.

"Tommy? Who was on the bridge? Who was on watch?"

"We were," replied Sid, pointing to himself and his brother.

"What about the radar? Don't tell me that's got belly ache too! Get down below the pair of you. Tommy and Mike can take the watch." He grabbed his stomach and, groaning, left the bridge.

"What a rotten trip this is," Cook grunted. "First the lad half drowns, then a mouse in my bed, nearly everybody throwing up and now a flippin' iceberg."

"Everybody throwing up are they Cook?" asked Stan Gallagher with a crooked smile as he left the bridge.

CHAPTER ELEVEN

Tommy and Mike looked at each other, but said nothing until everybody else had left the bridge.

"Why is everybody sick?" Tommy asked.

Mike thought for a second and said,

"I don't know. Do you think it might be food poisoning?"

"Food poisoning?" repeated Tommy. "But how? We've all been eating the same food."

The two boys thought for while before Tommy said,

"I didn't have the porridge this morning."

"Neither did I," Mike said thoughtfully. "Stay here a minute, I won't be long." He dashed out of the door.

While he was gone, Tommy continued on the same course and checked the radar. There were a lot of green blotches on the screen. He knew that if anything got close to the Stella Vega, he would see it straight away. Everything seemed to be at a safe distance, but he kept an eye on the screen anyway.

He didn't want to see another ice-berg close up again.

Mike came back puffing and panting.

"It must have been the porridge. The Gallaghers didn't have any, Cook and Brian didn't and neither did the second engineer."

"But how can you get food poisoning from porridge? It's supposed to be good for you. I always have it for breakfast in winter before I go to school."

"Unless somebody's put something in it?" Mike hinted.

"Who on earth would do a thing like that? Surely not? There was only Brian, Cook and me in the galley, and I didn't put anything in it."

"Cook wasn't very happy when he saw the hamster and he blamed you. And he didn't like it when the Skipper took your side," Mike suggested.

"Yeah, that's right," Tommy replied. "and Brian's fallen out with me. He thought I told Cook about the hamster. I said I didn't, but he wouldn't believe me."

Tommy and Mike took it in turns to steer the ship while the other checked the radar screen. It was nearly midnight when the Gallagher brothers returned to the bridge. Sid said,

"You two go down for a few hours sleep. We'll take over here. And don't worry, we'll watch out for ice-bergs this time." Patting Tommy's shoulder as he walked past.

Tommy left the bridge with Mike thinking those two looked very devious. They were obviously up to something, but what could it be? He thought carefully and remembered that a lot of the crew were poorly only a few days after setting sail. When they were safely back in their cabin he said,

"Mike, do you remember when everybody was sick on the third day out?"

"Yes, I remember. I thought it was strange at the time. Do you think it's got anything to do with everybody being sick this time?"

"I don't know," replied Tommy thoughtfully. "It might have been a trial run to see how it affected everybody."

Tommy didn't sleep well that night. People were continually running backwards and forwards to the bathroom, which wasn't very far from his cabin, waking him up every time he managed to doze off.

The next morning those who were sick were still in a bad way. Cook and Brian had spent most of the time running about after them and making sure they had plenty of water to drink. None of them wanted to eat anything, so Cook just made enough bread and fried a few fish for those who were still standing.

Tommy went to see his father. He had never seen him looking so pale.

"How's it going, son?" his father asked, worried about the ship.

"Alright Dad. We're managing. Mike and I take turns with the Gallagher brothers up on the bridge."

"The Gallaghers know what they're doing. They've been at sea for years."

Tommy didn't want to tell his father he didn't trust the Gallaghers. He would ask why and Tommy wouldn't be able to answer that question.

"Are you feeling any better, Dad?" he asked hoping for a positive answer.

"To tell you the truth," his father replied weakly

"I've never felt so rough in all my life. I can't think what's brought it on. Have you been alright?"

"Yes, Dad. I'm fine. I'll just get you some more water then I'll get off. Mike and I are due back on the bridge."

Tommy was steering the ship and pushing the bows over what was now a crisp, dark blue ocean with white horses riding over the crest of the waves. The sky was clear and the white, mountainous ice-bergs were at a safe distance. He was feeling a strong bond with the sea, like he belonged there and couldn't imagine ever being far away from it. It could be frightening at times, especially when it was very rough, but he respected it. He remembered he'd had a dream that had something to do with the sea before he came away, a dream that had scared him. What was it about?

He looked round the horizon and wondered why

he couldn't see any other trawlers. There had always been a few nearby the previous days. He asked Mike,

"Where are the other trawlers?"

"I don't know," Mike replied uncertain, and he also scoured the horizon. "Looking at our charts and the compass, we are heading east. Maybe we are just sailing around until everybody's better and we can start fishing again. The Gallaghers have set the course."

"Dad said they know what they are doing," Tommy added.

In the early afternoon, Tommy spotted a plume of black smoke on the horizon.

"Look, there's another ship over there," he shouted to Mike, pointing to the horizon beyond the bows of the ship. Mike took the binoculars and focused on the newcomer.

"It isn't a trawler," he said. "maybe it's just a merchant ship."

Both boys watched as the vessel slowly came closer, and it wasn't too long before they realized it

123

was a military ship. Tommy took the binoculars and focused on the flag it was flying. He could not mistake the red flag with a hammer and sickle in the corner.

"They're Russians!" he shouted. "I'm going to get the Gallaghers." He scooted down the stairs, bumping into the two brothers at the bottom.

"There's a Russian navy patrol boat and it's coming our way!" He yelled.

Sid bent down and with his nose close to Tommy's and whispered,

"Get back on the bridge and do as you're told. That way nothing will happen to you."

Tommy froze. This man was threatening him.

"Move," shouted Stan Gallagher, and Tommy flew back up the stairs again.

"Mike, they know. The Gallaghers know about the Russians. They said we've to do as we're told and nothing will happen. I'm going in to the radio room. I remember seeing how Norman talks over the air. I can get help."

"No, not yet," Mike replied nervously, "the

Russians might be listening in. We'll have to wait."

The Gallagher brothers were down on the deck as the Russian boat approached, and they signalled to Tommy to slow down. He pulled the lever towards him into the 'slow' position signalling to the engine room. Then they signalled to stop. Tommy and Mike looked at each other, both apprehensive of what was going to happen, before Tommy pulled the lever again to the 'stop all engines' position. The engines of the Stella Vega slowly ceased to pulsate and throb, and the ship just bobbed about on the sea like a cork in a choppy pond.

Cook came bounding up shouting,

"What on earth is going...." and seeing the Russian navy patrol boat closing in, said,

"Oh my word. What have we got here? Why didn't you come and get me?"

"The Gallaghers told us stay up here," Tommy replied.

All three of them looked down onto the deck where Sid Gallagher was standing in front of the fo'c'sle door as his brother came out carrying a box.

It wasn't a very big box, about the same size as a brief case, but it looked heavy as Stan struggled to lift it with both hands and place it on top of the hatch cover. He opened it, taking out some headphones and, after he placed them over his ears, he started twiddling some knobs with one hand and speaking into a mouthpiece which he held in the other.

"That'll be what they were doing that night I saw them on deck," Tommy announced.

"Yeah," said Mike, "I bet you're right."

"Well I never," said Cook dumfounded. Then he snarled,

"They're spies. They're nothing but a pair of dirty spies."

"The green book!" Tommy cried out remembering something important Norman had said to him one day whilst he was in the radio room with him, "I've got to hide the green book." He went in the radio room, then came out again and dashed down the stairs. Mike and Cook looked at each other and at Tommy as he raced off carrying the

126

book tightly under his arm and shook their heads as if the boy had gone stark staring mad.

Where was he going to hide it? It had to be somewhere safe where it wouldn't be found. He scuttled along the passageways trying to think straight when he remembered that aft, near the bathrooms, was a tiny little cupboard hidden away, low down, in a dark corner. That was a good place. No one would find it there. He lifted the latch and opened the door, but as he did so his chest became tight and the wheezing started. Brian's hamster! He threw the book inside, slammed the door shut again and, fighting for breath, crawled to his cabin to get one of his paper bags from under his mattress. He knew he had to get back up to the bridge quickly, so he concentrated really hard on breathing slowly in and out, in and out and didn't move until he felt strong enough to do so.

Tommy arrived back on the bridge just as the Russians were coming aboard.

"What was all that about?" Mike asked.

"I'll tell you later. But I've found Brian's

hamster."

"*Brian's* hamster?" Cook looked at Tommy scowling. "We'll talk about that later," and more urgently he continued, "Now, if these Russians ask you any questions you just say you don't know, both of you. Is that clear?"

"Yes Cook," Tommy and Mike replied together.

Stan Gallagher came up onto the bridge followed by four Russian sailors. They were all tall and thick-set, but one was bigger than the others. He had fair hair sticking out from under his cap, piercing grey eyes and a broad, potato-shaped nose that spread half way across his face. All four were carrying guns.

"Where is Capitan?" growled the big one who seemed to be in charge.

"He's sick," Tommy replied, only to be kicked in the ankle by Mike who was standing next to him. Stan Gallagher explained,

"Yes, most of the crew are sick. Must be something they've eaten," he added with a smirk on his face.

Tommy knew then that it was him or his brother who had poisoned the porridge.

"I want see capitan. Bring here now," the Russian growled again in a thick accent.

But just as he had finished speaking, Tommy's father came staggering onto the bridge gasping,

"Will somebody tell me what in the world is going on here?" Then he saw the Russians.

"You capitan?" asked the big Russian.

"Yes I am. What do you want aboard my ship? You're trespassing so I'm asking you to leave. Now."

"No Capitan. We no trespass," laughed the big man with the potato nose. Then sternly, "You trespass. You in Russian waters."

"What?"

"Sorry Skipper," Sid Gallagher stepped in smirking with his top lip curled upwards and a strange twinkle in his eyes, "we must have gone a bit off course."

"I want logs books," barked the big Russian.

"In the radio room," Sid Gallagher said pointing

them in the right direction.

"You'll pay for this Gallagher, both of you will," Tommy's father snarled trying to block the way, but two of the Russians who hadn't spoken grabbed him by the arms and held him up to the wall.

"Leave him alone!" shouted Tommy, jumping forward to stand in front of his father.

"Quiet small boy," threatened potato nose, this time holding his pistol in his hands. "Do what I say and you no get hurt. You make trouble and I shoot." Cook grabbed Tommy by the shoulders and pulled him back whispering,

"Do as you're told lad."

Sid Gallagher escorted potato nose into the radio room and Tommy could hear them rummaging around, flicking through pages and throwing books onto the floor. Tommy heard Sid pleading,

"I know it was here, I saw it with my own eyes."

"Stupid man," shouted the Russian impatiently.

"Find book now."

Norman staggered onto the bridge looking a bit grey and drawn.

"What's up?" he asked, then he saw the Russians.

"Where is book?" shouted the big Russian.

"What book?" Norman asked as he noticed Tommy wink at him.

"I no stupid. I want book with ships."

"I don't know what book you're talking about," Norman said adamantly, before running off the bridge with his hand over his mouth, ready to be sick.

Both Sid and Stan were accompanied by two of the silent Russians as they were sent to search the ship for the missing book. Everybody on the bridge waited in silence as they were watched by those steely grey eyes. Tommy was scared and felt helpless but prayed they wouldn't look in the small cupboard. If only he could tell his father that the book was safe. He felt sorry for his father who looked very weary. He looked down onto the deck where there were other Russian sailors standing guard and holding rifles. There were no other ships in sight, only the deep blue sea, and the distant icebergs. The situation seemed hopeless. What would happen to them? They could all be shot, or taken to Russia as prisoners. No one dared to speak as they waited. Tommy had never seen real guns before, only in films, and seeing them in real life made him nervous.

After what seemed like a very long time, the Gallaghers came back with their escort. There followed an angry sounding exchange between the Russians. Potato nose, frustrated, then turned to Tommy's father saying,

"We go. You lucky. You go from Russian waters." He left the bridge followed by the other three sailors and the Gallaghers, Stan pleading,

"Wait a minute, you can't leave us here, we're coming with you."

"You want come Russia? You sure? You lie to us!"

"We didn't lie. We saw it. Honest we did. We can't stay here now. We'll be arrested."

"Oh yes. You arrested. Come," with a penetrating, ice-cold voice, beckoning the brothers to follow and away they went, much to the relief of everybody on board the Stella Vega.

Cook, seeing that the Skipper was still not feeling well, helped him into the chart room and sat him down on the sofa.

"Phew, that was close," Mike said wiping his brow with the back of his hand. "What were they looking for?"

"A few days ago I saw Norman entering some figures in that green book you saw me with. He said if anybody found it we'd be in serious trouble. That's why I hid it. I'll go and get it."

"No," said his father. "leave it where it is until we're out of Russian waters. Now, let's see where we are so we can get out of here fast. Mike, come and help me with the charts, Tommy take the wheel, Cook, go round and check that everybody's alright."

Soon they were on the right course and they could see the Russian patrol boat steaming off in the opposite direction.

"What'll happen to the Gallaghers now?" Tommy asked.

133

"I've seen this happen before," Cook replied solemnly. "They probably think they'll live happily ever after, but they won't. They'll be taken somewhere to be interrogated first, then who knows where they'll end up. Those Russians weren't happy they didn't find what they were looking for."

Exhausted, Tommy's father went back to his cabin to rest and everybody breathed a sigh of relief as they sailed away at full speed to safer waters. Tommy went with him to make sure he settled and had plenty of water to drink.

"You did a grand job there lad. Good thinking. I'm proud of you."

Those few words meant the world to Tommy. He had made his father proud.

CHAPTER TWELVE

Tommy and Mike stayed up all that night, carefully following the new course the Skipper had set for them and taking it in turns to rest for a while on the Skipper's sofa in the chart room. Shortly after midnight Cook came up to the bridge with a fresh pot of tea.

"Right," said Cook. "Where's Brian's hamster?" With everything that had happened, Tommy had forgotten about the hamster. He looked at Cook with his mouth slightly ajar, just managing to stammer,

"Erm...erm..."

"I've seen Brian and he's told me all about it. Just wish he'd put me in the picture when he came on board instead of all this secrecy. Go and get it for him, will you. The daft lad's bawling his eyes out."

"I can't."

"What do you mean you can't?"

"I can tell you where it is, but I'm not going to get it. He can go himself." Not wanting to remind them of his asthma.

"Alright, alright. Just tell me."

The next morning the Skipper and most of the crew were up and about again, feeling much better. They were safely out of Russian waters and just a couple of hundred miles off the North Cape of Norway. It was as though the past couple of days had been nothing but a bad dream. Tommy's father was back on the bridge, Norman was back in the radio room communicating with the company back in Hull to inform them of what had happened, and the Mate and Bosun were down on the deck with a few deck hands. Once the hamster was safely in its cage in Brian's cabin, Tommy went to get the green log book and took it to Norman in the radio room.

"That was quick thinking Tommy lad, good job you remembered what I said. If those Russians had got hold of this we'd have been in big trouble."

"What's it for?" Tommy wanted to know more about it.

136

"Nothing for you to worry yourself about. Just a record of shipping movements. Now, how about a nice cup of tea?"

Norman wasn't going to say any more about the book, but Tommy thought that the shipping he was keeping a record of must have been Russian shipping. He wondered if his father knew anything about it. He would ask him some time when things were quiet.

Cook and Brian were busy in the galley baking bread and frying fish and Tommy made sure the teapot was always full of hot, steaming tea for whoever wanted it.

Brian got his hamster back and was allowed to keep it in his cabin, as long as it stayed in its cage. Cook didn't like the idea of little furry things loose around the ship. Tommy and Brian were friends again and even Cook had changed his tune towards Tommy. He had stopped calling him 'daft lad'. The crew were back on their feet and checking that the gear was in good shape and doing any small repairs that needed to be done. Once again, the

137

country and western music was blaring out over the loud speaker and some of the men sang along as they worked. Tommy took his turn at the wheel and looked down on the deck at those rough, strapping men. But, no matter how tough they looked, they still got the belly ache the same as everyone else.

The Gallagher brothers were never mentioned again. They had put the ship and everybody on board in danger and no one would ever forgive them.

CHAPTER THIRTEEN

The weather took a turn for the worse, but they had to start fishing again. They had lost so much time through food poisoning, sickness, storms and the Russians. They were now two men down having lost the Gallagher brothers, so Mike was promoted to Deck Hand and Tommy was to operate the winch, working eighteen hour shifts like the rest of them.

The Stella Vega was being tossed from side to side and up and down the heaving, swelling mountains, those fierce, live monsters that fought to take a hold of the ship. The engines groaned as she was pushed to the top of a wave, and there was a massive thump and a tremor as she landed down in the valley below over at the other side. Again and again, all through the day. The ocean was boiling and exploding beneath them and the crew tried their best to steady their legs so as not to fall. Some lost their footing and were swished from one side of the deck to the other, banging and thumping against whatever lay in their path, grunting as they hit and shouting out in pain.

Someone occasionally yelled "Water!" at the tops of their voices and everybody, Tommy included, grabbed hold of whatever they could so as not to be washed away by the deafening, booming, roaring sound of the rogue wave as it crashed down over the ship. Tommy had learnt his lesson that first time when Sid Gallagher had saved him from going overboard.

Tommy had been given some cotton gloves to wear, but they weren't much use. His hands were sore and blistered and he cried out every time he had to pull a lever or turn a handle or a wheel. His arms, his shoulders and his back were aching and his muscles were burning. His face was wet, he tasted the salt water in his mouth and, although he squinted, his eyes stung with the spray. He had to keep an eye on the Mate and listen and watch for his instructions, which were hard to understand through the howling wind. The Mate's instructions had to be acted upon straight away, no time to stop and think about it. The winch controlled the steel cables that were attached to the net and when it was set in motion, they quivered and strained and everybody moved away from them so as not to get hurt.

The wind was icy cold and stabbing Tommy's face with hundreds of tiny, sharp needles. He wore his oilskin frock and sou'wester to keep him dry, but there was no protection for his face. He couldn't turn his head away because if he did, he might have missed the instructions. Hour after hour Tommy stood at his post and did as he was told. Watching out for the Mate's next orders. Watching the deck hands squelching through the fish in the pounds as they picked them up, gutted them and tossed them below. All the time squinting and blinking the salt water from his stinging eyes, and groaning as his tired aching body moved to control the winch.

When his shift was over and a deck hand came to relieve him, Tommy could hardly move his legs one in front of the other. Holding on to the railing to stop himself from falling over, he made his way inside to the drying room. Mike was already there and helped him lift his oilskin frock over his head understanding the pain Tommy was in.

"It was hard for me the first time, but I got used to it. Look at my muscles now," Mike laughed holding up his arms and making a fist. "Come on, let's get some grub."

Tommy was too tired to speak and he was too tired to eat. All he wanted to do was lie down in his bunk and sleep, but he knew he must eat something if he was to carry on working. He made his way to the mess as though he was sleepwalking and plonked himself down on a bench at one of the tables. Not fish again? But he was hungry – very hungry, and he gobbled down everything on his plate before dragging himself to his cabin and his bunk.

"Wake up. It's our watch." Mike was shaking Tommy's shoulder as he spoke.

As Tommy woke he tried to stretch.

"Ow!"

He ached all over. How long had he been asleep? It couldn't have been very long as he was only allowed six hours to eat and sleep. He was still in his clothes. Good. It would save him having to get dressed. After a fish sandwich and a mug of tea, he put on his frock and went back to his post at the winch, much to the relief of the deck hand who had been standing in for him.

The weather was still filthy, but Tommy pulled himself together and stood ready and waiting for the Mate's orders. As the hard, laborious day wore on, conditions became even worse and the crew became exhausted in no time. It was so bad, it took the men twice as long to get the net in and shoot it again. By mid afternoon the Skipper decided enough was enough so he gave the order to haul in the gear for the last time. Everybody showed signs of relief, but nobody could slacken off until everything was back on board fastened down and the fish was in the hold.

The last haul was lifted above the pounds. Tommy

heard a strange noise of metal grinding against metal and suddenly someone cried,

"Look out!"

which was followed by a chilling, ear-piercing scream that turned Tommy's blood cold in his veins.

"Winch off NOW!"

someone yelled and Tommy did not hesitate to knock the lever bringing the winch to a grinding halt. In a daze, not understanding what was going on, he looked up and saw the cod end was swaying over the deck still tightly tied and hundreds of fish were flapping and wriggling inside. It looked like a bag full of giant maggots. The bridge window opened and somebody shouted up to the Skipper,

"Deckie's hurt!"

Tommy leapt forward to where there were a group of men kneeling on the deck.

"Mike," he shouted, and again "Mike! What's matter with him? What happened?" Searching the faces of those around him.

"Stand back son," the Mate said, "We've got to

get him inside to see how bad it is."

Tommy's father appeared,

"What happened?" he asked concerned.

The Mate spoke,

"Cable gave way and whipped right across him. We'll see what damage has been done when we get him inside."

"Get that fish in and sort the gear out," the Skipper instructed the bosun.

"Tommy, come and help us carry Mike inside, here, grab his feet."

Tommy's heart was beating fast and his hands were shaking as he grabbed Mike's ankles, trying to hold on tight and not let go.

Mike, unconscious, was carried to the mess where he was placed on a table. Cook arrived with a large knife and sliced though his frock to get it off him as quickly as possible. There was a lot of blood coming from Mike's right arm and Tommy moved his glance from Mike's motionless body to his father, Cook and the Mate who were looking down in amazement.

Cook cut open Mike's sleeve so they could see the extent of the damage. His right arm was still attached, but only just, and it was bleeding heavily. Tommy could smell the warm blood flowing out of Mike's arm and it made him feel sick. The Skipper took some bandages from a first aid box on the shelf and made a tourniquet above the cut to stop the bleeding.

"Get him in his bunk and pack as much ice round there as you can and give him some morphine – he'll need it," the Skipper instructed, "I'm going to call Hammerfest, we should be there in about seven or eight hours."

Tommy had never before heard his father sound so upset. Cook shook his head,

"By he was lucky. It could have been his head." There was a brief moment of stunned silence.

"Go and get ice, a bucket full," Tommy was told and off he went without asking why. He was glad to get away, yet glad to do something to help.

By the time Tommy returned with the ice, Mike was already in his bunk. Cook filled a pillow case

146

with the ice, placed it gently round Mike's injured arm, and said he would send Brian for some more. He left the cabin mumbling something about putting a pan of shackles on as the blokes would be hungry when they came in off deck.

When they were left alone, Tommy whispered to Mike to wake up and on doing so, Mike began to stir. He groaned and tried to sit up.

"Don't move." Tommy put his hands on his chest to keep him down. "You've had an accident. You've cut your arm." He didn't want to startle Mike by telling him how serious his cut was. "You're going to need a few stitches so we're going to Hammerfest in Norway where they can sort you out at the hospital."

Mike attempted a smile, but closed his eyes and drifted off to sleep.

Brian came with more ice and, after the crew finished putting the gear away on deck, they came by, one at a time, to ask how Mike was doing. All of them crept about and whispered quietly so as not to disturb their injured crewmate.

Meanwhile, the Stella Vega headed towards the Norwegian coast and the weather seemed to be calming down, making it easier for them to go full speed ahead. Mike continued to drift in and out of consciousness and while he was awake, Tommy chatted to him about anything but his accident. He talked of some of their neighbours in West Dock Avenue, he talked of their local football club, Hull City, The Tigers, about the bad season they had just had and hoped the next one would be better. He told him that Brian's hamster was safely locked in its cage in his cabin, but the poor thing didn't have a name. He asked Mike if he could think of a name for it and he suggested 'Cookie'. They both laughed then Mike asked,

"Are you enjoying your trip?"

Tommy was taken by surprise and not knowing how to reply said simply,

"Is it always like this?"

"Yeah. Except for the Russians. We don't get them every time we're up here." And dozed off to sleep again with a strained grin around his mouth, trying to hide his pain.

Tommy was up all night taking care of Mike who was very clammy and his skin was a pale shade of grey. At times he woke up for a while and sometimes mumbled a few words or shouted and tried to get up. It took all of Tommy's strength to hold him down. Cook came in a few times to change the ice bag and see how he was doing. At about four o'clock in the morning, his father came down to tell him they were docking in Hammerfest and an ambulance was on the quayside waiting for them.

"The Mate's going ashore with him. Do you want to go too?"

"Can I Dad? Will it be alright?"

"Yeah. I'm sure he'd like to know you're there."

Mike was carefully transferred to the ambulance, the Mate and Tommy behind carrying his kit bag with his personal belongings. They waited a couple of hours sitting on hard wooden chairs in a cold, stark corridor before a doctor came out and beckoned for the Mate to go with him. Tommy remained seated and waited. After about half an hour, the Mate came back his face looking grim and drawn. He put a hand on Tommy's shoulder, and whispered,

"Mike's operation went well, but we have to leave him here. Come on, let's get back on board, your Dad'll be wanting to know what's happened."

In silence they sat on the back seat of the taxi that took them back to the ship. It was half past seven in the morning. Everybody was up and about and they all wanted news of Mike. The Mate went straight to the Skipper's cabin and the door closed behind them. The Skipper called all the crew to the mess, but first wanted to speak to Tommy on his own.

"What is it Dad? Is it about Mike?" Tommy was afraid of what his father was going to say. He could see it was bad news by the grim expression on his face.

"Yes son. The doctors did their best, but they couldn't save Mike's arm."

"Do, do you mean they cut his arm off?" Tommy stammered taking a step backwards and reaching out to steady himself and not fall over.

"Yes, son. I'm sorry. You can stay up here for a bit if you like. I've got to go and tell everybody else. Be brave. Remember what a brave lad Mike is."

"Who'll tell his Mam and Dad?" Tommy asked wondering how they would find out what had happened to their son so far away from home.

"I've contacted the company back in Hull," his father said, "they'll let his family know. When we get home I'll go to the house myself. I sailed with Albert Beech, his dad, a few years ago and they're nice people. It's a shame." He shook his head and repeated, "A shame." He left the cabin.

Tommy was alone and he did something he had not done for a very long time. He sat on the floor with his back against the wall, pulled up his knees and hugging them tightly he lowered his head and cried. His father had told him to be brave. He didn't know what being brave really was. He was brave when he went to the dentist's. He was brave that time he fell off a wall and broke his leg. But

151

this was a different kind of brave and he didn't understand.

CHAPTER FOURTEEN

The Stella Vega had to wait for the next high tide before sailing from Hammerfest and that wouldn't be until about five o'clock that evening. The mood on board was subdued and the air felt heavy. Everybody seemed unsettled and restless. There was a card game going on in the mess, and Brian and Cook played a game of draughts.

"Do you want a game?" Brian asked Tommy.

"Not just now thanks," he replied and left the mess to go and stand out on the deck, to be alone, as he felt stifled inside.

The sun was shining brightly, but there was a chill in the air. After all, they were still within the Arctic Circle. The buildings were very different to those in Hull. There were some offices and warehouses around the harbour, but they were not made of brick like those back home. They seemed to be made of concrete or wood. It wasn't as busy as St Andrews Dock, although there were signs of movement with a few people walking about and the odd truck moving along the roads. There were some fishing boats, smaller than the Stella Vega, and various other boats too.

Most of the houses were made of wood and were painted different colours like red or blue or cream, and all the window frames were painted white. They were spread out and dotted along the coastline and a little inland. Some of the houses closer to the water had boats tied up outside. He noticed a church spire. The church was made of wood and was painted white. Beyond the town, Tommy could see mountains with signs of snow on the peaks, but they were not rugged mountains like the ones in the Alps he had seen in pictures in his school books. These mountains were much smoother and rounder, and he noticed there weren't any trees. The landscape beyond the town was, in fact, quite barren. He was wondering how deep the snow was in the winter when he was shaken from his thoughts by Cook's unusually soft voice,

"Come on lad, there's jobs to be done."

Tommy followed Cook inside thinking, 'he didn't

call me daft lad.' They found Brian with a bin of taties. Did Brian ever change that grubby apron?

"Shall we do this outside, like we did when we sailed from Hull?" Brian was doing his best to be nice. He had been told that Tommy hadn't told tales on him and felt ashamed that he hadn't trusted him. He was sorry about what had happened to Mike. He had seen accidents on board a few times before, but Mike was only sixteen, and to have lost his arm at such a young age was an awful thing to happen. What would he do now? He wouldn't be able to go to sea any more.

"Yeah, let's. I'll bring the stools," Tommy tried to sound cheerful.

Although Tommy and Brian chatted to each other while they peeled the taties, a melancholy cloud hung over them. They would be sailing that evening and leaving Mike behind, in hospital in a foreign country, all alone.

Later that evening, Tommy stood on the bridge with his father and asked,

"How will Mike get home?"

155

"When he's well enough to leave hospital, the agents will arrange for him to get to Bergen where he'll be put on the post boat to Newcastle and he can get the train to Hull from there. That's what usually happens." He turned to go to the radio room to talk to Norman.

Tommy tried to imagine what the journey would be like for Mike, travelling alone, not understanding the language. The doctor in the hospital spoke English and so did the shipping agents, but the people he'd be travelling with wouldn't. He would go and visit Mike when he got home.

His father returned to the bridge.

"Norman says we're going to be hitting some pretty rough weather later tonight. There's a right old storm brewing up out there."

"It's all my fault we've been having bad weather, isn't it Dad? It's because I whistled I brought the bad weather."

"Now don't you go thinking that because it isn't true. It was your first time at sea. You weren't to know. And anyway, it doesn't count the first time, so just get it out of your head. Now, go and find the Mate and find out what needs doing. You take your orders from him because you're the Deckie Learner from now on."

"All the way home?"

"Yes, son. All the way to St Andrews Dock."

Tommy was delighted. He had a proper job to do. A real man's job. He skipped off the bridge and ran to his cabin to put on his sea boots and oilskin frock before going to look for the Mate.

As the Stella Vega prepared to sail, Tommy stood on the fo'c'sle with one of the deck hands, ready to pull in the ropes and secure them for the voyage. He felt ten feet tall once again.

"Ready to go Deckie?" asked the deck hand.

"Ready to go," Tommy responded with a twinkle in his eye.

Sailing through the Soroya Sound towards to Norwegian Sea, Tommy took a last glimpse of Norway. There was the island of Soroya on the starboard side and Seiland to port. What a strange land, he thought. No trees to be seen anywhere, only brightly painted little wooden houses dotted along the coast and up the hillsides. He looked up at the sky and saw that it was looking very dark on the horizon. Norman had said they would be running into some bad weather, but those clouds looked very angry.

After tea, he sat in the officers' mess with his father, the Mate and Norman.

"Well Tommy," asked Norman, "what do you think of your first trip to sea? Will it be your last?" Tommy had been expecting this question at sometime, so he cleared his throat and said,

"I would like to do it again."

His father looked anxious as he said,

"Do you mean another pleasure trip?"

"Yes," hesitating slightly before continuing, nervously looking sideways at his father, "and I would like to go to sea when I leave school." There. He'd said it.

"Fishing?" His father was stunned.

"No. Yes. I don't know," Tommy stammered.

"You don't want to go fishing lad," his father

sounded disappointed. "You're a bright lad. You passed your Eleven Plus exams. I can see that all this is new and exciting for you. I want you to think very carefully about it. You never know, you might change your mind before you leave school."

Tommy felt deep inside that he wouldn't change his mind. He definitely wanted to go to sea somehow. He already knew the connection he felt with the sea would stay with him forever. But he wasn't going to try to convince his father yet. It was going to take time to bring him round to his way of thinking and he had to find out how he was going to do it.

CHAPTER FIFTEEN

No one on board slept that night. It was the worst weather of the whole trip. Everybody was on edge and seemed to be on stand-by, as though they were waiting for something to happen. The tense atmosphere made Tommy nervous and the noise was deafening. Apart from the howling wind outside, the bang and thump of the waves crashing against the ship, there were also doors that had not been secured slamming open and shut. In fact, anything that was not fastened down rolled backwards and forwards clattering and banging as it went. Tommy played a few games of draughts with Brian in the mess and asked him how the hamster was doing, adding,

"Mike said you should call it 'Cookie'"

Brian laughed out loud flashing his crooked teeth,

"Yeah, that's a good idea. Cookie. It's a good name." He laughed again remembering all the fuss when Cook found the hamster in his bed.

It had been a long night. When dawn broke,

Tommy carefully made his way to the bridge, holding on to whatever he could to stop himself from falling over. Even before he got there he could hear the wind screeching through the rigging, much louder than the last time. It now sounded like an angry, ferocious wild beast. The Bosun was at the wheel and the Skipper was standing close by. Tommy looked out of the bridge windows and, at first, all he could see was the colour dark green. Dark green, swirling sky matching a very angry, dark green sea, all repeatedly lit up by frequent flashes of fork lightening. The sky was growling, the sea was growling. The waves were enormous. Much bigger than the ones he had seen before. There had been huge waves when making their way north and when they were fishing, some of them as big as mountains. But now, the whole of the sea around them was like a moving range of mountains, mountains that were continuously changing shape and size, mountains that were alive. The Stella Vega was, at first, sitting in a deep, dark trough, in the jaws of the beast, surrounded and dominated by huge walls of water on all sides, then balancing on top of the crest ready and waiting to be transported into the groaning depths once more. Many of the waves smashed against the bridge, making it shudder and shake as though it would be knocked off the ship. The Bosun held tightly onto the wheel as the Stella Vega slid down the vertical slope into the valley below. It was like being on a giant big dipper that takes your breath away, only much more intense. Then up they went again, thrusting and straining, only to be completely covered from forward to aft by the next wave. They were taking a right old battering this time.

Tommy was holding on tight with both hands, his eyes nearly popping out of his head, hardly believing what he was seeing.

"Don't worry son," his father said trying to reassure him, "I'll get you home again. We're sailing as close to the coast as we can, but we've hit the tail end of a hurricane."

"A hurricane? I thought they only had hurricanes in America?" Tommy asked.

"They do," his father confirmed, "as I said, it's the tail end. Hurricanes often travel across the Atlantic Ocean, but they're weaker when they get over here."

Tommy thought if this was weak he wouldn't like to be in a full blown hurricane. He looked out again and saw that some of the ropes and cables between the mast and the derrick were flapping about loosely. He pointed them out to his father.

"Yes, I know son, but we can't do anything about it yet. It's too dangerous to go out on deck. We'll get it fixed when we're in calmer waters."

So, Tommy looked helplessly on as wave after wave came over them, battering and lashing as the Stella Vega thrust forward, up and down, up and down, rolling from side to side, engines screaming. Behind him, in the radio room, he could hear Norman talking on the radio and at the same time the morse code was di di da-ing again.

Tommy's father asked him what he had learnt about hurricanes at school, and Tommy was only too pleased to tell him all he knew. They also talked

163

about other subjects he studied and Tommy was delighted his father was taking an interest and, not only listening to what he said, he was asking questions too. But as they spoke, both were fully aware of the danger they were in, and neither of them took their eyes away from frightful scene outside.

The next wave hit so hard, it smashed through two of the bridge windows sending broken glass flying everywhere and the sea water gushed in soaking them all and swilling about on the floor. Luckily, Tommy was unscathed, but the Bosun had a cut on his forehead and the skipper's arm was bleeding.

"Dad!" Tommy shouted as he jumped over to where his father was standing.

"I'm alright son. I'm alright. What about you Bosun?"

The Bosun, still holding on to the wheel replied,

"I'm alright, it's just a scratch."

There was nothing to stop the waves coming through and swirling about on the bridge. Tommy, his father and the Bosun were soaked through to the

164

skin and cold. Yet they battled on, Bosun at the wheel, Skipper checking charts and compass and Tommy, broom in hand, trying to push the water out onto a platform just outside the bridge.

By late afternoon, the tempest was beginning to subside. The sea was still rough, and waves were still pounding the deck, but the sky had turned grey instead of the threatening dark green it had been only a few hours earlier. The Mate arrived on the bridge,

"We've still got a few hours of daylight left so I think I'll get that gear fixed before we lose it altogether. I'll need the Deckie Learner to give us a hand."

"Right you are," the Skipper said, "Off you go Tommy lad."

There were four of them working on the deck; The Mate, Tommy and two deck hands. One of the hands was up the mast securing the gear and another was below him steadying the ropes and cables. The Mate was looking on giving instructions and Tommy's job was to do the

165

fetching and carrying of any tools they needed, as well as to keep an eye on the sea to look out for rogue waves. Tommy was now used to being out on the wet, slippery, deck that rolled and shuddered beneath his feet, riding the ocean waves. He turned to look up at the bridge where he saw his father at the window smiling and waving at him and Tommy smiled and waved back, thrilled at the close bond that had grown between them.

Tommy saw that the sky was turning black again towards the horizon and there were flickers of lightening. He told the mate who glanced in the direction Tommy was pointing and said,

"We'll be finished by the time that lot comes over."

Nevertheless, Tommy felt uneasy. There were stronger gusts of screeching wind and he saw the sea was once again turning a spooky shade of green. The dark waves were splashing around them on the deck, becoming bigger and more frequent. He looked over the starboard side and saw a huge swell heading their way. He promptly shouted,

"Water!"

166

as loud as he could, but as the word came out of his mouth, he saw a heavy cable with a large metal hook at the end of it, swinging round, heading right for the Mate.

Tommy leapt forward and just managed to push the man out of the way as the wall of water hit them. Tommy lost his footing and was picked up by the wave and propelled along with it.

The great frothy, foamy hands of the watery giant wrapped themselves around him and dragged him down. Fighting for breath, he was gasping, spluttering, and thrashing his arms. He tried to scream, 'Help!', but his mouth filled with the icy cold salty water as he was spinning round and round. He went under, then came back up, and went under again, kicking his legs and wrestling to get back up again. His clothes were heavy, tugging him under, swirling down in the vortex, but he carried on fighting, even though he felt the strength seeping out of him. A voice inside was yelling, "Dad! Dad!" Down, down he sank, ever deeper into the black depths of the abyss.

Quote

'He sinks into thy depths with bubbling groan,
Without a grave, unknelled, uncoffined and
unknown.'

Byron: Childe Harold's Pilgrimage

Unquote

His boots became loose and he managed to shake
them off making it easier to kick. He came to the
surface again and felt a tight grasp on his arm.
Someone was helping him, pulling him up out of
the water and shouting,

"Swim Tommy, swim!"

A lifebelt had been thrown overboard and Tommy
swam towards it. He missed the first attempt at
grabbing hold of it, but reaching out as far as he
could, he managed to get a strong grip the second
time. The lifebelt was attached to a rope and was

being pulled towards the ship.

"Hold tight Tommy! Don't let go!" somebody was shouting. Then,

"Water!"

Tommy felt himself being lifted by the wave and carried forward towards the ship. He held tight onto the lifebelt, screwed his eyes up tight and gritting his teeth, he braced himself thinking he was going to hit the side of the ship. But instead, the wave lifted him over the side and dumped him on the deck with a great thump.

CHAPTER SIXTEEN

Tommy opened his eyes. He was no longer in the sea, no longer wet and no longer gasping for breath. He was lying in a warm, dry bed and his father was sitting by his side.

"It was my dream Dad," he gasped.

"That wasn't a dream son. It was a flipping nightmare. I thought we'd lost you."

"You don't understand Dad. It really was the dream I had the night before we sailed. It scared me, but I couldn't remember what it was." Then, after a few thoughtful seconds, Tommy continued,

"Did I really go overboard Dad?"

"Yes you did, but only because you saved the Mate from a nasty knock on the head."

Tommy closed his eyes and thought for a while, trying to remember what had happened. Then it all became clear.

"How is he Dad?"

"He's fine, but still in shock. When you knocked

170

him over he bumped his head and passed out. The spare hand was quick off the mark holding on to him so he didn't go over as well." He stood up.

"You try and get some sleep now. I'll come and see you later."

"Dad?"

"Yes son?"

"Was there somebody else in the water?"

"Yes son."

"Who was it? Are they alright?" Tommy asked slowly, almost afraid of hearing bad news.

His father stood in the doorway of the cabin and spoke with a croaky voice and a lump in his throat.

"It was me."

Father and son looked into each others' eyes for only a few short seconds, but that intense moment held a deep knowing that the bond they had forged made them as one, forever.

Tommy slept fitfully throughout the night, feeling the rocking and rolling and clanging, banging, thumping noises of the ship tossing about in the storm. He woke the next morning to a calmer sea and to find his father once more by his side with two mugs of tea in his hands.

"Wakey wakey Rip Van Winkle."

"Morning Dad."

"Get dressed and come and have your breakfast in the officers' mess."

Tommy did as he was told, feeling a bit wobbly, but much better than he felt the previous night. His father and the Mate were at the table eating eggs and beans. He sat at the table next to his father, opposite the Mate.

"All right lad?" the Mate asked.

"Yes, thank you."

"You did a very brave thing yesterday. Thank you."

"That hook was going to hit you," Tommy said.

"It would have if it hadn't been for you. You're a good lad." He took a long slurp of tea and left.

"We'll be home in a day or so," Tommy's father sounded relieved to be going home. "It's been a rotten trip, what with one thing and another. And we won't get much for the fish we caught so wages will be low. I don't know what your mother will say."

Mother. Tommy hadn't thought about his mother for quite some time and felt guilty. He tried to sound cheerful,

"I hope they had a good week in Withernsea."

"I'm sure they did son." His father smiled before continuing, "Are you coming up to take the wheel? We'll be sailing along the coast of Northumberland. You might be able to spot a few castles."

CHAPTER SEVENTEEN

The Stella Vega sailed south towards the estuary of the River Humber with Captain Tommy Ellis at the helm. He had changed. No longer was he the naive youth who fumbled and stammered as he arrived on board. Here he was, confident and brave and he remembered a poem he had learnt at school, written by a man called John Masefield:

Quote

Sea Fever

'I must go down to the seas again, to the lonely sea and the sky,

And all I ask is a tall ship, and a star to steer her by,

And the wheel's kick and the wind's song, and the white sails shaking,

And a grey mist on the sea's face, and a grey dawn breaking.

174

I must go down to the seas again, for the call of the running tide,

Is a wild call and a clear call, that cannot be denied,

And all I ask is a windy day, with the white clouds flying,

And the flung spray, and the blown spume, and the sea-gulls crying.

I must go down to the seas again, to the vagrant gypsy life,

To the gull's way and the whale's way, where the wind's like a whetted knife.

And all I ask is a merry yarn from a laughing fellow rover,

And a quiet sleep and a sweet dream, when the long trick's over."

Unquote

Glossary of Terms

Kerb - Raised ledge at the side of the road

Mate - Second in command of the ship

Bobbers - The men who unloaded the fish

Kit - Metal container used to carry fish

Daft - Dialect word meaning 'stupid'

Deckie Learner - Learning to be a Deck Hand

Taties - Pronounced 'tayties' – potatoes

Chow at - dialect word meaning 'reprimand'

Guernsery - heavy woollen sweater

Fearnought trousers - heavy, warm, work trousers

Tea mashing – tea brewing

Made in the USA
Charleston, SC
26 July 2014